PETTICOAT MARSHAL

When Buck Morgan's son is apparently murdered by a lawless drifter, the town of Willis Creek is thrown into turmoil. The townsfolk face financial ruin if Morgan's ranch takes its business elsewhere. Those who stand to lose the most decide that justice in the form of a necktie party will assuage the rancher's anger — but Marshal Abe Black stands in their way. When the badmen dispose of him, it is up to his daughter, the formidable Belle, to enforce justice . . .

JACK HOLT

PETTICOAT MARSHAL

Complete and Unabridged

LINFORD
Leicester

First published in Great Britain in 2001 by
Robert Hale Limited
London

First Linford Edition
published 2003
by arrangement with
Robert Hale Limited
London

British Library CIP Data

Holt, Jack
  Petticoat Marshal.—Large print ed.—
Linford western library
  1. Western stories
  2. Large type books
  I. Title
  823.9′14 [F]

  ISBN 0–7089–4921–5

Published by
F. A. Thorpe (Publishing)
Anstey, Leicestershire

Set by Words & Graphics Ltd.
Anstey, Leicestershire
Printed and bound in Great Britain by
T. J. International Ltd., Padstow, Cornwall

This book is printed on acid-free paper

To the memory of my parents
with loving thanks

1

Marshal Abe Black settled down to read the three-month-old newspaper sent to him by his sister Amy in Boston, with the ususal letter pleading with him to hand in his badge and come East with Belle, his daughter and only child — not that she was a child at twenty-two. Her banker husband, Charles, would provide employment for them both in the bank of which he was president.

'That badge will get you killed one day, Abe,' Amy had warned again.

It annoyed her that her younger brother, by two years, was not prepared to heed her advice. She was the kind of woman who wasn't used to getting or taking no for an answer. Their father had been shot in a poker game in a Yukon tent-town when Abe was twelve and Amy fourteen, and she had virtually taken over the running of the family, their mother, rest her soul, having been broken in spirit by her husband's untimely demise. Though why she should grieve so over a rogue and vagabond like Danny Black, no one could understand — least of all her daughter.

Black's reading was interrupted by the sound of gunfire, and with an ear used to judging gunshot distance, he murmured, 'The Jug o' Grog.' It wasn't uncommon for a ruckus to break out in Willis Creek's premier saloon on a Saturday night — in fact any night. Black waited a couple of seconds. If there was no follow-up, Sullivan, the owner of the Jug o' Grog, would have cracked a few skulls together and restored order. The County Cork man, built as big, raw and rugged as one of that county's black-faced mountains, was such formidable opposition that most hardcases' ambition to create mayhem wilted when he showed.

As the second and third volleys rang

2

out, Abe Black put aside his newspaper, swept back thinning black hair, donned his Stetson, buckled on his gun and headed for the saloon at the south end of town. He was beginning to tire of what was becoming a nightly trip to one or the other of the town's drinking, gambling and cathouse establishments, the setting up of which he had strictly opposed at the town-council meeting that voted in, the year before, what the council called Willis Creek's more liberal living style.

Jack Roycroft, the council chairman, town banker and a finger-in-every-pie sort of fella, made fun of Abe Black's pleas to keep Willis Creek the kind of family-orientated community that it had been for the twenty-four years of its existence.

'The town needs to expand, Abe,' was Roycroft's answer to his objections. 'The town that stands still dies.'

He had done his homework well, holding out the temptation of greater trade and fatter bank balances to his fellow councillors to undermine the marshal's anticipated objections.

'This is a family town, gents,' Black had continued to press. 'A safe town for folk to go about their business in peace.'

'Business, Abe,' Nat Gentle, one of Willis Creek's founding fathers sighed, 'we've got less and less of, while Oakville is getting more and more.'

Oakville was a wild and open town about twenty miles north of Willis Creek. Its marshal was the see-nothing-hear-nothing kind of fella that gave honest lawmen a bad name.

Jack Roycroft had piped up. 'The thing is, Abe, if we want to stay in existence as a town we need trade; that means folk coming to Willis Creek to conduct their business . . .'

'Some kinds of business we'd be better off without,' Abe Black had stated bluntly, and became even more forthright still when he added. 'Whoring and drinking every hour that God gives isn't my idea of the kind of business Willis Creek needs.'

For a brief moment Nat Gentle rowed in behind Black.

'Abe has a point, gents. The decision we take today decides what kind of town Willis Creek will be tomorrow.'

Roycroft, seeing the indecision that Gentle's much respected views brought to the proceedings, was quick to stoke his fellow councillors' greed.

'There's a whole lot of trade to be gained and a whole lot of pockets to be filled if we liberalize our laws. Times are changing. We change with them or go under. It's as simple as that.'

This point of view got a whole lot of head-nodding.

Angered, Black had put in. 'And who gains most from a booming town, huh? The bank, that's who. And that's you, Roycroft.'

Roycroft chuckled. 'You're a real stick-in-the-mud sort of man, aren't you, Marshal.'

'I've got values that are not for trading,' Black responded grimly.

'What's wrong with the town prospering, Abe?' a small wizened man called Art Wood asked.

'We got mouths to feed, Abe,' another man had said.

'You don't want the town to fold up, do you, Abe?' a third councillor had pressed the marshal.

'If that happens, you'll be out of a job as well,' Art Wood had reminded Black.

'I haven't got any objection to the town attracting new business,' Black countered. 'It's the kind of business that worries me. We don't need any more saloons, the one we've got is adequate for our imbibing needs. And we certainly don't need a cathouse, like that fancy one over in Oakville — '

'Why, Abe,' Roycroft slipped in with snake-oil smoothness. 'You seem to know a whole lot about Oakville's cathouse.'

This had the councillors sniggering, until Nat Gentle doused their mirth with a fiery tirade.

'There's no call for snide remarks or

sneaky laughter. Over the years Abe's kept us safe in our beds at night, and on our streets by day.' He took the centre of the floor to pronounce: 'We've got a whole lot to be thankful to Abe Black for.'

Roycroft, feeling the mood swing against him, poured oil on troubled waters.

'Nat is right.' And turning to Black, he apologized to the marshal. Nat Gentle's rebuke had stirred the consciences of the other councillors and Roycroft feared that if he pressed for a vote right then it would probably swing against him. Craft and cunning were weapons that had served the banker well. He saw no need to ditch them now. 'Maybe it would be best if we all went our separate ways and gave both the marshal's and Nat's remarks some thought. What say you all we meet again in a week's time?'

He had played his hand well. There was a general murmur of agreement, and the town councillors were more than glad to disperse. He'd use the week's grace to work on them privately, and was confident that, come the next council meeting, he'd have no trouble.

Abe Black, a foxy fella, recognized the banker's ploy for what it was — a strategic withdrawal to allow him the time to whisper in the ears of doubters, and twist the arms of those beholden to him, of which there were many, with the town's trade in the doldrums since the opening up of its neighbouring town to the kind of Sodom and Gommorah antics going on there.

A week later the town council voted in favour of Jack Roycroft's proposal to back-pedal on the strict code of conduct that had, in Abe Black's opinion, made Willis Creek a family friendly place to live in.

Approaching the Jug o' Grog, a couple of the Big M outfit were spilling from the saloon, shooting their guns in the air and engaging in general drunken antics. The giant-sized Joseph Sullivan came from the Jug o' Grog and began tossing the troublemakers around like he might straws, knocking heads together. Abe, certain that Sullivan would restore order, was about to turn around and head back to the law office, when a gun flashed in one of the rooms above the saloon and a man came crashing through the window, bouncing off the porch overhang, before landing on the flat of his back in the street among the horses hitched to the rails outside the saloon. Excited by the scent of fresh blood, the horses kicked and stamped on the man, but it didn't make any difference to him. With half of his face blown away, Randy Morgan wasn't feeling the animals' stomping hoofs. A second gunblast sent a saloon-dove, name of Linny Bates, the same route.

Sprinting up the saloon steps, Black ordered Sullivan: 'If the killer tries to escape through the window, shoot him if he doesn't stop!' As he crashed through the saloon door, Andy Stoddard, a relative newcomer to Willis Creek, and a regular visitor to Linny

Bates, was rushing downstairs, green eyes blazing like a trapped animal, threatening the saloon's patrons with a smoking six-gun, and headed for the back door that led to the town's dark backlots.

'Hold it right there, Stoddard!' the marshal snapped. 'You be sensible now, and drop that iron you're brandishing.'

A clear pathway opened up between the two men as the saloon's patrons dived every which way to seek cover from what looked like certain gunplay.

'It ain't my doing, Marshal,' the young man pleaded. He glanced at the pistol in his hands. 'This ain't mine!'

'You're holding it,' Black said stonily.

'You've got to believe me,' Stoddard whined. 'I didn't shoot Randy Morgan, nor Linny Bates.'

'I'm prepared to listen, son,' Black said, calming the young man's nerves. 'But first you've got to hand over that Colt.'

'Randy? You've murdered Randy?'

Stoddard, alarmed by the sudden

wave of belligerence that swept the saloon, pulled back the gun he was about to hand over to Black. Luke Barrow, the foreman of the Big M Ranch, and the man who'd just spooked Stoddard, stepped forward.

'He's killed Randy. String the murderin' bastard up.'

Panic, as swift and devouring as wildfire, gripped the young man. His eyes reflected madness as a mob from the Big M surged forward. He fired the gun, his jittery hand thankfully sending his shot harmlessly into the air, but it had the effect of scattering the mob, and again left a clear path between Black and the suspected killer.

'Drop the gun, son,' Abe Black coaxed. 'Tell your story.'

'Yeah,' screamed Stoddard. 'And who the hell's going to listen to what I've got to say, Marshal?'

'I will,' Black promised him, his grey eyes reflecting the honesty of his answer.

After a moment's consideration,

Stoddard said. 'Even if you listened to me, Marshal Black, how long do you think I'd last in your jail, before I was hauled out and strung up?'

'There'll be no lynching in my town, Andy,' Black promised.

Barrow, a man with a stirrer's instincts growled, 'We'll get you, Stoddard! No matter what the marshal promises you.'

Black back-handed the Big M foreman, sending him crashing over a table.

'Whose side are you on, Marshal?' another Big M, ranny groused.

'Ya see,' Andy Stoddard whined. 'I ain't goin' to git no fair hearing in this town, Marshal Black.'

Barrow, black pebble eyes glaring, was back on his feet and prodding for trouble. 'We all know how sweet you was on Linny Bates, Stoddard. Used to visit her regular!'

'Yeah. You're right, Luke,' the town drunk chanted, licking parched lips and seeing the Big M ramrod as the source of his next drink.

'Go on with your reasoning, Luke.' A lanky galoot who now and then took the notion to work and cleaned out Stafford's livery, encouraged the Big M foreman.

Backing growing, Luke Barrow went on:

'I figure that tonight, when Stoddard called, Linny was pleasurin' Randy and he didn't like it none. So, he upped and gunned him down outa pure spite.'

'It ain't so,' Stoddard protested.

'Barrow's reasoning makes sense, son,' Frank Burton, the owner of the mercantile store, stated.

Abe Black tried to calm Stoddard's hiking panic.

'You have my word, Stoddard,' he turned to say his piece to the assembled gathering, 'that I'll shoot the first man who even tries to sling an unlawful rope on you!'

The crowd, in the main now supporting Luke Barrow's view of the way things had panned out upstairs, grumbled and growled at what they saw as their marshal favouring a clear-cut killer, against the overwhelming wishes of the town's citizens.

Frank Burton spoke again.

'You're not making yourself very popular Abe, supporting a no-good like Stoddard.' His blunt statement brought a chorus of approval from the crowd. 'And with an election in the spring . . . '

Riled by Burton's veiled threat, Abe Black replied stonily. 'Are you saying, Frank, that I should implement the law on a mob's whim?' His steely eyes drifted over the crowd. 'Mob law is no law. And the law in this town, as long as I'm marshal — '

'Which ain't goin' to be for long more,' Barrow interjected.

Black ignored the stirrer's jibe, and finished. 'Is going to stand by the principle that a man is innocent until proven guilty.' His challenge now was aimed directly at the mercantile store owner, who was also a town councillor and had been a supporter of Jack Roycroft's liberalizing crusade. 'And if any man wants to take issue with that, he can cast his vote against me come election time. Or . . . ' Abe Black changed his stance, 'he can take issue right here and now.'

No one had the grit to take up the marshal's challenge. He turned to Stoddard. 'Shuck the gun and come on down here, son.'

'There's only one damn way to settle this,' a Big M ranny growled, pulling iron and sending a bullet smashing into the wall alongside Stoddard.

Black's scowl was fearsome. Wound up, the ranny turned his gun on the marshal, whose pistol cleared leather in a spit and sent lead into the man's kneecap to disable him. Meanwhile, Stoddard, unnerved, cut loose, scattering the crowd.

'Damn!' Black swore, and vaulted the stairs' bannister to land a pile-driving fist in Stoddard's face. It sent him tumbling down the stairs to sprawl on the floor. Black was quickly on top of him. Stoddard fought like a caged mountain cat, snarling, spitting and gouging.

'Someone get some cord and tie his hands,' he ordered.

No one responded.

Burton said: 'There's nothing much a fella can do with a mad dog but kill it, Abe.'

'Turn him over, Pa.'

Black looked up to see his daughter holding a curtain cord. Belle Black, in lightning-quick time, had Stoddard trussed up like a Thanksgiving turkey. Task completed, Black asked, 'What the hell are you doing in a saloon, Belle?'

She smiled, showing even white teeth, the smile going deep into her hazel eyes. 'Doing my civic duty, helping the marshal.' As she turned to face the crowd, her chilliest look went Frank Burton's way. 'Like any good citizen should.'

'We have a prisoner to get to the jail,' Black said, proudly placing his arm around his daughter's shoulders.

Luke Barrow led the sniggers. 'Just as

well there was a woman on hand to help you, Marshal.' The Big M foreman's sneer vanished under Abe Black's hammer solid fist. When he picked himself up at the other side of the saloon, Barrow snarled, 'You're building up a real passel of trouble for yourself, Black.'

Black glowered. 'Any time you want to unwrap that passel, Barrow, you just come looking!'

The crowd piled out of the saloon on their tails, and others came to swell it as Abe and Belle Black marched Andy Stoddard to the jail. As they progressed, Barrow and his cronies drew together the threads of what had happened in the Jug o' Grog for the citizens who had only recently joined the commotion, adding their own biased embellishments, until, by the time Abe Black reached the jail, the crowd had become a mob howling for Stoddard to be strung up.

On reaching the marshal's office, Black promised: 'If a judge and jury says that's the way it's going to be, that's the way it will be. But not before Mr Stoddard has his chance to tell his story.'

'Buck Morgan ain't goin' to stand for this kinda nonsense, Black,' Luke Barrow railed.

Uncompromising in his stance, the marshal intoned: 'Mr Morgan, like everyone else, will have to await the jury's verdict.'

Barrow vaulted into leather, and before he rode off at a breakneck pace hollered: 'We'll just see 'bout that, Marshal.'

'Go on home!' Black ordered the mob.

Slowly the crowd dispersed, some lingering longer than others in open and hostile defiance.

'Are you going to be able to hold out, Pa?' Belle asked, when Black came inside the office, worry dulling her hazel eyes.

'Not without a good deputy, I reckon.' He sighed heavily. 'I'll have to sleep some time.'

'Then get a deputy,' Belle said.

He snorted. 'It isn't that simple, Belle. You see, no one wants the damn job.'

2

In the back room behind the mercantile store, Frank Burton was addressing a hastily convened meeting of business-men who, if Buck Morgan were to withdraw his support, would lose a stack of shekels.

'I think that Marshal Black has overstepped the mark, gentlemen. This town simply can't do without Big M business.'

'It surely can't,' Jack Roycroft, the town banker, supported Burton. The banker stood up to take the floor. 'Buck Morgan is the biggest spender in this neck of the woods. And we can't . . . ' he paused to let his gaze drift over the assembled traders, 'and won't, allow Abe Black to ruin this town by his stubborn attitude. The way I hear it there's no doubting Stoddard's guilt. So, I'm with you in saying that swift justice should prevail.'

Though Frank Burton was glad to hand the lead to Roycroft, it suprised him that the always cautious banker's support for Stoddard's hanging was so whole-heartedly forthcoming.

'What if he ain't guilty?' All eyes fixed on the massive form of Joseph Sullivan, the Jug o' Grog's owner. 'Well, it ain't a fact for sure,' he said defensively, defying the hostility going in his direction. 'I come from a country where too many men were hanged on a whim, for lynchings to settle with me easy-like.'

'Do you want to see this town fade off the map, Sullivan?' Roycroft said, scorn for the ill-educated Irishman twisting his smooth, almost feminine features. Folk said that he got regular shipments of a fancy French face-cream shipped in on the stage every couple of months, along with a French pomade to hide the grey in his hair.

'Andy Stoddard's as guilty as hell,'

Roycroft pressured the Irish saloon owner. His pale-blue eyes, as cold as arctic ice, bore into every man in the room, before he finished: 'And should be strung up right now for Randy Morgan's murder.'

Sullivan had a whole lot to say about that, being opposed to the idea of impromptu hangings; believing that a man should have his day in court before a rope was slung, but his words dried up under Jack Roycroft's sneering superiority. When it came to fighting, Sullivan would break a man's skull without qualm. However, when it came to the intricacies of reasoned argument, his shortage of words and how to put the few he had together, was an impediment that shackled his tongue to the roof of his mouth.

With Sullivan's objection silenced and the meeting going Roycroft's way, the banker continued:

'I say we should send a citizen's deputation to see the marshal. To let him know how this community feels about him acting as Stoddard's protector.'

This suggestion brought a chorus of approval from the meeting.

Roycroft volunteered: 'I, if you kind people agree, will lead the citizens' deputation.'

The banker got whole-hearted support, because there were very few at the meeting who relished the idea of facing up to Abe Black. He was a no-nonsense, pickaxe-blunt sort of man, who never kept his views to himself, and never appreciated any interference with the implementation of the law. A good man and a fine friend to have on your side. But a thorny, hard-hitting opponent to have to face.

Roycroft got a free hand in picking the three-man delegation, deciding that Frank Burton, the mercantile store owner, and Wes Shine, the town lawyer, friends and fellow travellers of Roycroft, would be the town's spokesmen.

A weedy man at the back of the room suggested: 'Maybe it would be best to have Stoddard at the end of a rope before Buck Morgan rides in. Might take the sting out of his spite.'

'Makes sense,' Frank Burton agreed.

The weedy man's suggestion proved a popular one, except with Joseph Sullivan. He almost voiced his objections, but that was before Jack Roycroft glanced sneeringly his way and he lost courage, not wanting to be made a fool of when Roycroft threw in a couple of hundred-dollar words that made no sense to him.

★ ★ ★

Belle Black went to the law office window on hearing the commotion on Main, to see Jack Roycroft leading a sizeable crowd to the office.

'What's going on out there, Belle?' Abe Black enquired, coming from the cells. He was holding Andy Stoddard's account of what happened upstairs at the Jug o' Grog.

'Looks like you're about to have a

town delegation coming through your door,' Belle told her father. 'Led by Jack Roycroft!'

The marshal's face soured. He had never taken a shine to the banker who had come to town three years ago, and he reckoned he never would.

'Well, no prizes for guessing what they want, I guess,' Black intoned. He plonked into the chair behind his desk, just as Roycroft led Burton and Shine in — Shine having to force the door shut to keep out the press of people behind him.

3

'Gents,' Black greeted the town delegation. 'What can I do for you?'

Roycroft snorted. 'I think you know the answer to that, Marshal Black.'

Abe Black's features set grimly. 'Tell me anyway, Roycroft.'

The banker scowled. He had never appreciated what he considered to be Abe Black's disrespectful manner. 'You've got a killer in your jail that the town wants hanged.'

'Right now,' Frank Burton put in.

Black's steely gaze came to rest on Shine. 'You're a lawyer, Wes. You know the law. So, what the hell are you doing being party to breaking it?'

Shine squirmed and claimed lamely: 'Everyone knows that Stoddard shot Randy Morgan, Abe.'

Roycroft scoffed. 'You caught him holding the smoking gun, Marshal.'

'Because a man is holding a smoking gun, doesn't mean he did the shooting. If that was the way of things, there'd be a whole lot of unjustified hangings in the West.'

All eyes went Belle Black's way. Burton was first to react to the surprise interjection.

'This isn't business proper to a young lady, Belle.'

'Yes,' Roycroft intoned. 'You should be at home making apple pie, Miss Black.'

There was nothing as sure-fire as male arrogance to fire up Belle Black's temper. She defiantly tossed back her head of coal-black hair, an inheritance from her father, and her hazel eyes glowed dangerously. 'I'll decide what I'll do,' she declared. 'And I'll have no man deciding for me. Even a darn banker!'

The visiting trio looked to Abe Black for prompt chastisement to be delivered. There was none forthcoming.

'Belle's always had a mind of her

own, gents. And I wouldn't have it any other way.'

Jack Roycroft's colour was rosier than a setting sun. 'Are you going to stand against the town's will and continue to protect that killer?' he demanded of the marshal.

'I guess that's the size of it, gentlemen,' replied Black.

It was Frank Burton's turn to get uppity. 'The town might not think you fit to hold office, Black.'

'Don't matter none until next April. That's when I come up for re-election. And seeing that this is only September, I figure that one way or the other, long before then, Stoddard's fate will have been decided by due process.'

Jack Roycroft complained: 'There might not be a travelling judge reach town for months. Do you think Buck Morgan is going to stand around doing nothing?'

'The law applies to every man equally,' Black said uncompromisingly. 'And that includes Buck Morgan!'

Frank Burton, seeing that threat and intimidation were not going to work, switched to a honeyed approach.

'You're not going to be a very popular fella around here, Abe,' his glance took in Roycroft and Shine, 'and we wouldn't want that.'

Burton's partners, quick to adapt to the change of approach that the mercantile store-owner had initiated, agreed whole-heartedly.

'We surely wouldn't, Abe,' Shine crooned, nervously.

'We don't want any acrimony, Marshal Black,' Roycroft added pleasantly.

Abe Black's smile was lazy and knowing. 'Then don't come marching in here trying to strong-arm me!' he grated. Then standing up, ramrod straight, he declared stonily. 'This meeting is over, gents!'

Rattled by Black's brash rebuff, Burton ranted. 'Another thing. What're you going to do about the Changs?'

'What about the Changs?' Belle quizzed her father.

Abe had not told her about the Pure America Committee that had been formed by some of the town's leading citizens, three of whom formed the delegation to his office. Jack Roycroft, a Southerner from Alabama had been the motivator in setting up the organization. The committee's aim was to make Willis Creek the kind of town where people like the Changs would not be welcome, in the hope that other towns would follow their lead. The committee had pressurized Black to make the Changs leave town; a pressure he'd steadfastly refused to yield to.

Roycroft took up Burton's challenge. 'The Pure America Committee think it isn't proper for the marshal's daughter to be on such friendly terms with the Changs, Abe. Gives the wrong impression. It could encourage others like the Changs to settle in Willis Creek.'

Belle flared. 'I'll choose my own friends. And I'll not be asking your permission!'

'The Changs aren't breaking any

laws,' Black stated. 'I don't have any grounds for chasing them out of town.'

'The Changs are not like us,' Frank Burton railed. 'Isn't that reason enough?'

'We've got Irish and a Pole. And there's that Italian over in Clancyville. And a couple of Germans in Oakville,' Belle pointed out.

'Belle, be quiet,' Black ordered his daughter. The fact was that, much as it unsettled him, Abe Black did not see a Chinaman as being the same as an Irishman, a Pole, German or Italian. And it nagged his conscience. He cringed under his daughter's bewildered glare.

'Chang says he's a Buddhist.' Wes Shine sneered. 'Whatever that is.'

'I asked him last Sunday if he was going to church like the rest of us good folk,' Roycroft said. 'He told me he didn't believe in Christianity.'

'A man is entitled to find his own route to heaven,' Belle stated.

'We have a duty to convert the

heathen, Miss Black,' the banker intoned loftily.

'Mr Chang is not a heathen!'

Wes Shine shrugged, and shook his head as if he was dealing with an obstreperous child.

'Belle — '

'That'll be Miss Black,' Belle snapped.

'There isn't any call for brazenness, Belle,' the marshal rebuked her.

Shine went on. 'The fact is, *Miss* Black, that anyone who does not believe in God must be a heathen.'

'Your God,' Belle said.

'That's quite enough, young lady,' Black reprimanded his daughter.

But Belle Black was in no humour for parental chastisement. And at twenty-two years of age, she reckoned that she had a right to her own opinions, and the right to state them, too.

'Sullivan and Dolan are Irish Catholics,' she argued with Shine. 'They don't go to church — *our* church.'

Belle was stunned when it was her

father who answered her challenge.

'Sullivan and Dolan believe in the same God, Belle.' He chuckled. 'It's just that the Irish, being of an argumentative nature, would have to have their own version of him.'

'If that's so, don't the Changs have the same right?' She challenged the quartet of men.

Jack Roycroft laughed indulgently. 'I swear I don't know what ideas your daughter's got in her head, Abe.'

'My own!' Belle flung back.

Frank Burton put a direct question to Black. 'Are you going to run the Changs out or not, Marshal?'

Belle looked to her father as he pondered Burton's question, and feared what his answer might be and what her opinion, afterwards, of the man she loved and cherished would be. She'd always thought her father to be a fair and just man, and she hoped she was right.

'We understand your dilemma, Abe,' Shine said smoothly, 'Belle being really friendly with the Changs. But we figure that you wouldn't want your daughter . . . well, let's say tainted by their strange beliefs and customs.'

Black was in a quandary. Shine had stated correctly his worry about his daughter's association and growing friendship with the Changs. He'd tried a time or two to raise the matter with Belle, but had never found the right words. The fact was, while not fully supporting the aims of the Pure America Committee, he could neither, in honesty, say that he saw Chang as being the same as Sullivan or Dolan, or the Pole with the unpronounceable name who farmed just outside of town. However, as a lawman he was sworn to uphold the law and the rights of the town's citizens, including the Changs, and that he'd do.

He pronounced: 'I reckon Chang and his family have the same rights as you and me, gents. And my or your views, if different, don't enter into it. I'll not take kindly to any man who makes the

Changs unwelcome.'

Belle Black flew into her father's arms and hugged him. Abe did not feel wholly comfortable with his daughter's adulation. He would have to clear the air, and soon, and explain the distinction between his official duty as a lawman, and his personal views as a man. It was a task that he was not looking forward to.

That booklet he'd found on Buddha in Belle's room had come as a real stunner. He'd said nothing about it, but he'd been fretting. His daughter wasn't a kid any more. Handling a woman, particularly one as feisty, independent and opinionated as Belle was no easy job.

Roycroft was first to recover. He settled mean eyes on Belle Black.

'I truly hope that you won't live to regret the stance you've taken, Abe.'

Me, too, Abe Black thought.

'I think that concludes our business, gents,' Black said.

The banker sneered. 'It concludes

this meeting, Marshal Black. Not our business.'

'No, sir,' Frank Burton growled.

As the door closed behind the delegation, Abe Black murmured. 'I never reckoned it had.'

★ ★ ★

Buck Morgan never liked his reading habits to be disturbed, having been taught to read by his Bostonian wife only a few years before, when the Big M had become what Buck Morgan wanted it to be, and he could turn his attention to other things. He had taken to reading books fervently, and, being sixty-three years old, there were a lot of books to be read in the short time that he reckoned he had left. He'd been waking nights, breathless, and most days ended with a tightness in his chest that he knew would, in shorter instead of longer time, prove fatal.

He was, after many years of fighting and upheaval, as he carved the Big M from the untamed country he'd settled in all of forty years ago, a contented man. He missed Ellie, his late wife, and wouldn't quibble with God when the time came to be reunited. He had the compensation and consolation of their son Randy, a man with a lot of his mother in him. Randy had his wild ways but Buck reckoned he'd settle well and soon. The rancher reckoned that when the time came, he'd be passing the Big M into very capable hands.

When Luke Barrow burst into the study to interrupt his reading, he warned: 'This had better be urgent, Barrow. Or I'll skin you alive!'

He spent a minute listening to what Barrow had to say, and five minutes more taking it in, with every one of which his heart and spirits sank lower and lower. He took a deep breath to keep his staggering heart going and, putting aside the book he was reading, stood up. Grimly, he said. 'Saddle a horse for me, Luke. I've got a hanging to go to!'

4

Abe Black handed his daughter the statement he'd taken from Andy Stoddard before the arrival of the town delegation.

'The words might not have the letters in the right order,' he said, 'but you'll have no trouble getting the gist.'

Abe Black was a mighty proud man that Belle Black was called on by a lot of the townsfolk whose reading and writing skills were pretty sketchy, if not downright absent completely, to read their letters and write their answers, often marvelling at the fancy words that Belle came up with.

Belle occupied her father's chair to read Stoddard's version of Linny Bates's and Randy Morgan's murders — Linny Bates being the dove that Morgan was lying with when the crime was committed. It began with the accused man's visit to the saloon. As she read, pausing every now and then to decipher her father's spelling, Belle Black's eyes became wider and wider until she exclaimed: 'Linny Bates was Andy Stoddard's sister?'

Black took up the part of Stoddard's story that was not in the statement, but which he'd told to him.

'Stoddard's story is that Linny and him were separated as kids, during the trek West. An Indian attack finished off most of the settlers, and the tatters of what remained formed new families, taking on the orphans as their own, sometimes to replace offspring they'd lost themselves. Not an uncommon practice in those dangerous times.

'Both the Stoddard elders were killed in the attack, so Ike and Mary Bates, Christian folk to the core who had lost their little girl in the skirmish, took the six-year-old Linny Stoddard, as she then was, to rear as their daughter, while another couple took the four-year-old Andy under their wing. Fifty miles on the wagon train divided, as a lot of wagon trains did, burdened as they were with sorrow and dissent. Linny and Andy Stoddard took different trails; Andy to Montana and Linny to Arizona.'

'How did they meet up again?' Belle quizzed, not sure if she was as ready to believe Stoddard's story, as her father apparently had.

'By pure chance, as happens in the West. Andy Stoddard was working on a river boat plying the Mississippi, selling his considerable weight and muscle to fellas who'd struck a winning streak at the tables, to make sure that they survived long enough to reach dry land and enjoy their winnings. The Mississippi yields up a whole lot of *hombres* with slit throats and empty pokes.

'Well, one day, as Stoddard was napping on deck, having gone through an all-night vigil outside one lucky gent's cabin door, a young lady stumbled over his outstretched legs and went sprawling on the deck. Stoddard, being a gentlemanly sort, went to the woman's assistance and to collect the items that had spilled from her bag. One of those items was a gold locket which he readily recognized, due to the fancy engraving of a bird on its cover, put there by Arthur Stoddard's hand. Stoddard senior was a goldsmith. Andy opened the locket and instantly recognized the picture of the child inside as his long-lost sister, Linny.'

'That,' Belle Black pronounced, 'is a mighty heart-tugging story, Pa!'

'But is it true, huh?' He smiled.

'You reckon?' Belle asked.

After a moment's consideration, Abe Black opined: 'Well, Belle, hearing it as I've told it, I've got to admit that it sounds as green as an Irish shamrock, and a yarn that a whiskey-thirsty Irishman might spin, but if you were there at Stoddard's telling, you'd probably, like me, figure that there was more truth than yarn in his story.'

'If you believe it,' Belle said, 'you not being a man easily fooled, Pa, then I guess I'll throw away my pinch of salt and row in with you. If,' Belle Black squared her shoulders, 'your story about how Linny turned up here three years before Andy Stoddard holds water. Seeing that they had this great and joyous reunion on the Mississippi.'

Before continuing with the tale related to him by his prisoner, Abe Black rolled a smoke, fired it up and sat for a spell pulling on the weed, before responding to his daughter's impatient urging to finish Andy Stoddard's romantic tale.

'That night on the gambling-boat, Stoddard came a cropper. Having celebrated with Linny a mite too liberally, his senses were dulled somewhat, which allowed a bush-whacker to get the drop on him. He ended up in the great river with an egg-sized bump on his skull, and was lucky that the current took him to the river-bank rather than downstream. The client he'd been hired to protect lost his poke and his hide — ending up throat slashed not too far away from Stoddard.

'A couple of days after, when he caught up with the *Atlanta Queen* and searched for his sister, he found that she'd disembarked back along the river on the arm of the silk-vested gambler whom his client had won his pot from.

'Stoddard isn't that bright a spark, but it didn't take many marbles to figure out that he'd been set up, and the sole purpose of his sister's ensnaring of him was to dull his senses with liquor and make him an easy target for the Fancy Dan she was with, to dent his skull and slit his client's throat.'

'Tell me, Pa. Can Andy Stoddard read well?' Belle enquired.

Abe Black pointed to the statement she was holding. 'He signed that. Why?'

'Because his story sure sounds like one of them dime-novel plots that the general store gets a batch of now and then.'

Black nodded in agreement, and

chuckled. 'It gets even hairier still, Belle!'

Belle sighed. 'Let's hear it.'

The marshal continued his narration of Andy Stoddard's story.

'Stoddard was in a mighty mean humour, having been duped the way he had been, and having been fooled by his long-lost sister made him even more gallish. He searched for a year and a tad more, until he traced the woman he believed to be his sister to Mexico, to a cathouse for jaded whores, where the woman from the *Atlanta Queen* told him that she'd stolen the locket from another whore while she was working in a travelling wagon-brothel, pleasuring miners, prospectors and railroad builders and any other dregs that happened along. With Stoddard thinking she was his long-lost sister, the Fancy Dan, seeing the possibilities of a quick flush of cash, got her to play along with his quick-riches scheme.

'From her, Stoddard got Linny's last port of call. Starting from there he arrived here in town nigh on a year and a half later to find his real sister working as a dove at the Jug o' Grog. Shamed, he asked Linny to keep their kinship quiet.

'He didn't much like the idea of his sister working as a saloon siren. So he resolved to free her of her way of life, and took to gambling to get the shekels for the grandiose plan he had of moving on with Linny, where his brawn could be put to good use on the docks of San Francisco. He'd heard there was good money to be made there for a man with his kind of muscles.

'The only flaw in Andy Stoddard's plan was, that he wasn't too bright at cards and lost more often than he won, which had him drifting into petty crime to get the next couple of dollars to go back to the card tables.

'Linny, being in a more lucrative business than her brother, took to funding him, which explains his frequent visits to her room at the Jug o' Grog. With him having sworn Linny to secrecy, it looked like Stoddard was Linny Bates's best customer.

His arguments with her, which folk put down to jealously because she wasn't granting him exclusive rights, were nothing more than Linny resisting her brother's growing demands, as his debts at the gambling tables mounted.'

Abe Black drew in the last of his smoke, and opined: 'I guess, not knowing the facts like we do, Belle, it's easy to see how folk are picking Andy Stoddard as a sure bet for a rope. The picture of him finding Linny in bed with Randy Morgan spiking his jealousy is a mighty powerful and plausible one.

'And if I can't prove to the citizens that, as he claims, Stoddard was waylaid as he entered Linny Bates's room in the dark by a hooded figure who shot Randy Morgan and Linny Bates, and then stuck the smoking gun in his mitt . . . well, I reckon that Stoddard will swing for sure!'

'There isn't a doubt about it,' Belle Black agreed.

5

The meeting that had taken place earlier in the back room of the mercantile store had now moved to Jack Roycroft's sumptuously furnished parlour, but had lost in number and gained in exclusivity. Ben Charles, the town mortgage-lender, had been added to the trio of Roycroft, Burton and Shine, who had formed the delegation to Abe Black.

For all practical purposes these men ran Willis Creek. If you needed goods hauled in, Frank Burton saw to it. If a body broke the law, he called on Wes Shine's advocacy. For a loan, a man needed Jack Roycroft's goodwill. And if you had a loan on your property, you kow-towed to Ben Charles.

The only people free of these men's influence, with the exception of one man, were in pine boxes in the funeral parlour or the cemetery.

That one man was Abe Black.

The quartet, fearful of earning Buck Morgan's wrath, and anxious to keep the wealth that the Big M ranch generated in the town, most of which ended up in their pockets one way or another, were more desperate than ever to present the rancher with Stoddard swinging on a rope, as recompense for the killing of his son.

The Big M boss would be mad as hell with the town, was the quartet's conclusion. But if, when he rode in, Stoddard was swinging in the breeze, it would go a long way to curbing Buck Morgan's anger.

They hoped.

'And how the hell do you expect that to happen?' Ben Charles asked. 'With Abe Black standing in the way!'

There was a long silence in which each man had his own thoughts. Only one expressed them, but Jack Roycroft suspected the rest of them had much the same thoughts he had.

'I figure the only way to get a noose around Stoddard's neck in time is to, ah . . . ' his gaze went to each man in turn, '*remove* any impediment to that end, gents!'

Frank Burton gave Roycroft his instant support. 'Figures!'

Wes Shine was less enthusiastic, though not outrightly condemning, while Ben Charles was cautious.

'Killing the marshal could bring all sorts of grief,' he advised.

'Like?' Roycroft quizzed impatiently.

'Like putting a US marshal on our doorstep!'

'If no one talks,' Frank Burton growled, 'then there'll be nothing for a US marshal to hear, will there?' His eyes bored belligerently into the mortgage-lender. If he lost Buck Morgan's patronage, he might as well pack up and leave town.

Ben Charles had good reason for not wanting a US marshal in town. Lawmen of that calibre had a worrying way of burrowing deep into a man's past, and he had a past which, if tested, would be as unsound as a holed bucket. Things could come to light: facts like Charles not being his real monicker, and facts like the mysterious disappearance of a partner he once had down Arizona way. Facts, too, like that gent's emptied bank account. No, sir. He did not want a US marshal anywhere near Willis Creek.

He fretted. 'There's no real need for any killing, is there?'

Roycroft's and Burton's angry scowls expressed their displeasure at the mortgage-lender's foot-dragging. He was a fly in the ointment that made Roycroft curse his invitation to him to join them. Wes Shine's hesitancy, too, he could do without.

Tight-lipped, Roycroft grated: 'Knowing what kind of a stubborn cuss Abe Black is, have you got another way, Ben?'

Charles, desperate that he'd be forced to be part of Roycroft's and Burton's crazy plan to murder Abe

Black, not that he'd ever lost any sleep over murder, pressed on.

'Killing a lawman is never a smart thing to do, Jack.'

'So, what's your plan, Ben?' Burton enquired starchily.

'Maim him. He'll still be out of the way long enough for us to give our man the star. A quick trial and everything will be over before you know it.'

'Our man?' Shine asked.

Ben Charles's suggestion brought a smile to his fellow connivers' lips.

'Luke Barrow, I reckon, would be a good choice for marshal.'

'You know, Ben,' Roycroft sneered, 'you're smart enough to run this burg on your own!'

Charles quickly scotched any idea of his usurping the banker's clout in town.

'I'm happy enough to just have a finger in the pie, Jack!'

This assertion brought a round of hearty laughter.

When the laughter died, Burton said: 'We've got plans to make, gents!'

Belle Black, not for the first time, had gone to the law office door to look across the street at Jack Roycroft's imposing house, pondering on what might be going on in that *hombre*'s parlour. She feared the outcome of the meeting of the town's most powerful figures now taking place. Her father had made light of their earlier visit, but Belle wasn't so sure that the trio would take his stance lying down. Now, with Ben Charles added to their camp, she was even more certain that they would challenge Abe's decision to hold out for a trial for Andy Stoddard. If all went well, there was a travelling judge due any day, but in the tinder-dry atmosphere following Randy Morgan's killing, an hour had become a long time in Willis Creek.

By now Buck Morgan must know of his son's murder. His wrath, added to the plot-hatching quartet in Roycroft's parlour, could make Willis Creek a mighty unhealthy place for a principled lawman like Abe Black to live in.

Turning from the window, she said: 'You need a deputy and fast, Pa.'

'I told you, Belle. No one wants the job.'

'I know of someone who'd take it.'

Abe Black's interest perked up.

'You do? Who?' Her wide grin had him leaping out of his chair. 'Forget it, Belle!'

'Why? Because I'm a woman?'

'That, too,' Black yelped. 'I never heard of anything so loco in all my life!'

Belle promoted her cause. 'I can shoot straight.'

'There's more to being a lawman than shooting straight.'

'I know the law backwards, Pa.'

'That still isn't enough!'

'And I can hold my own in a fight, too.'

'A cat-fight, maybe. But there's a whole world of difference between hair-pulling and the kind of bust-up that breaks out in the Jug o' Grog, or the other watering-holes in this burg.' Father and daughter glared at each other, before Abe Black sighed. 'Hell, gal. Why didn't you inherit your mother's sweet nature instead of my ornery one.' Abe drew his daughter into his arms. 'It just isn't a job for a young lady, Belle.' His tone became warm and soft. 'Besides, you're all I've got now, Belle.'

★ ★ ★

In an alley close to the marshal's office, Jack Roycroft was on an errand of evil.

'You looking for me, Mr Roycroft?'

A man came out of the shadows; Roycroft's heart staggered. He was not a brave man, just a conniver who got other men to do his dirty work for him, like the man he'd come to meet. Luther Harding was a lazy no-good who spent his days sponging instead of seeking honest work, picking up a couple of dollars wherever and whenever he could, and not being too particular about how he got his mitts on them. The banker had used him a couple of times before for his nefarious deeds.

'Must be kinda 'portant for you to be creepin' 'round alleys at night, Mr Roycroft.'

Harding's voice held a note of insolence that raised the banker's hackles, but he stifled his angry retort — there was urgent business to be taken care of, and Harding was the only one that he could trust to put his proposition to.

Roycroft spoke in whispers, his eyes constantly scanning the pitch-black alley and the street beyond. His story finished, Harding grinned broadly.

'It'll cost ya,' he told the banker.

Roycroft shoved a bundle of dollars in the layabout's hand.

Harding fingered the bills and said: 'Kinda thin, I reckon.'

'There's fifty dollars there,' Roycroft grumbled. 'All you've got to do is put Abe Black out of action for a spell.'

'The thing is,' Harding sighed, 'When

the deed is done, I'll have to leave town, lie low for a spell. And that costs, Mr Roycroft.'

Over a barrel, the banker was resigned to being bled.

'How much?'

Luther Harding's grin widened.

'Two hundred?' he tested.

'A hundred,' Roycroft flung back.

'One seventy-five,' Harding returned.

'One fifty!'

Harding offered a hand that Roycroft had last seen up a saloon dove's skirt. The banker grimaced, and was careful when handing over the extra one hundred that Harding had demanded, to place the money in the hand that had been only around the dove's waist. He had dallied some himself but he was always careful to have Linny Bates visit him in the small hours at home.

'You'll arrange the ruckus in the Jug o' Grog?' Harding asked the banker.

'It's in hand.'

'Then,' Harding slid his pistol from leather and rolled the chamber, 'all we need is to get Black out of his chair and 'long to the saloon.'

Just then a man crashed through the Jug o' Grog's window, while another followed him through the door. Several more men staggered on to the saloon veranda, punching, kicking and gouging. Joseph Sullivan made an appearance, half a dozen men clinging to him, with one on his back trying to open his skull with a whiskey bottle. Sullivan shrugged the men off, hauled the man on his back over his shoulder and tossed him into the street. Coming down on his right elbow with the whiskey bottle in his right hand, he found it rammed into his face, shattering on impact to leave a jagged hole where the right side of his face should be. His howl echoed along Main. A couple of the men Sullivan had thrown off got second wind and got their skulls cracked together for their trouble. By now the saloon was one great big slugging parlour.

'Black's on his way!' Jack Roycroft

pulled back from the corner of the alley as he saw the marshal come from his office, and slipped away in the darkness to leave Harding to do his deed.

'You be careful,' Belle Black called after her father.

'I'm always careful,' he called back.

'Not careful 'nuff,' Luther Harding sniggered. In a couple of seconds Abe Black would pass the alley and get the surprise of his life. He thumbed back the pistol's hammer.

The marshal's ears pricked up on hearing what he thought was a gun being cocked, but he wasn't sure if he could trust his ears with the fury of the fight spilling out of the Jug o' Grog. A gun flashed, which changed the nature of the saloon fracas. Abe quickened his pace to the saloon, but there wasn't a chance of his making it.

Luther Harding had him in his sights.

6

A second too late, Abe Black caught the movement in the alley out of the corner of his eye. An orange flash lit the darkness. His right leg buckled under him as Harding's bullet smashed his femur, and he went down howling in anger and heart-stopping pain. As he crashed to the ground, his gun cleared leather and began spitting lead into the alley. A man cried out. Seconds later Luther Harding stumbled from the alley clutching his belly, trying to keep his innards from spewing out.

Jack Roycroft, watching in safety from the dark window of his unlit parlour, felt panic race through him; the elation of seeing Black go down seconds before, quickly evaporating as Harding came from the alley, mortally wounded, but standing.

'Shoot him, Black! Damn you!' he

whined. The last thing he wanted was for Harding to remain standing long enough for him to blab. Dying men invariably got the urge to confess.

Black waited. Right now Harding's gun was hanging limply by his side, and he didn't seem to have the spit to raise it. He forced down his urge for revenge. Harding was no threat now, and in his time as a lawman he had never over-used a gun, seeing an iron as a preventer of mayhem rather than an initiator. It was a view that, on a couple of occasions, had almost been his undoing, but one which he had resolutely stuck to.

Luther Harding's breath came in ragged gasps, and his glazed eyes rolled.

'It's over, Luther,' Black grimaced. 'We both need the services of Doc Forbes.'

'Ain't no doc goin' to do me no good, Marshal,' Harding gurgled, blood trickling from his lips. 'You got me good. I'm all done for.'

Black did not contradict him. He had

learned early that lying to a dying man was of no practical help. Harding's light was going out faster than a lamp in a storm.

The ruckus at the Jug o' Grog had come to a standstill, men who were at each other's throats only a minute before were now standing in reverent silence as a man died. Relieved, Roycroft spotted the low-life duo he had paid to hike the trouble in the saloon sneak away into the darkness.

'Why, Luther?' Abe Black asked his maimer. 'We haven't ever locked heads in no serious sense before.'

Jack Roycroft had opened his parlour window a slit, and in the hushed silence had clearly heard Black's question.

'Didn't think that bushwhacking was your style,' Black said to Harding.

'It ain't,' the bushwhacker replied in a dry rasping tone.

'Then why did you do it, Luther?'

Harding rooted in his pants pocket and came up with Roycroft's dollars. They blew away on the breeze as

Harding's body jerked and his fingers lost their grasp. 'You know what a hun'red and fifty dollars means to a man like me, Marshal?'

Sweat as thick as molasses covered every inch of Jack Roycroft's body. He glanced back to the Colt on his desk and swallowed hard. Should he risk trying to finish Harding off? He was a fair shot, but not a marksman, and his parlour window offered an acute angle relative to where Harding was standing. If he succeeded in felling his agent, he'd also get the credit for coming to Abe Black's assistance, which would raise his stock with the ordinary citizens of Willis Creek and do him no harm at all. On the other hand, if he missed, Harding would know of his treachery and turn his spite his way. Which would mean Abe Black heading his way soon after, mean as a mountain cat.

'Who paid the assassin's fee, Luther?' Black asked grimly.

'I was never goin' to ki-kill you, Marshal.' Harding sagged in the middle and fell to his knees, great clots of blood coming from his mouth. 'Ju-just put y-you outa ac-action.'

'Who put those dollars in your fist?' Black demanded. 'The grave can be a mighty restless place for a man carrying a hellish secret into eternity, Luther!'

Roycroft figured he was left with no choice. He had to risk shooting Harding, or face Abe Black's wrath. It really wasn't a choice at all. The banker was haring back to the parlour window, his pistol clenched in sweat-greasy hands, when a rifle shot rang out and he heard Abe Black bellowing, 'God dammit, Belle, what did you do that for? Why the hell din't you stay out of it?'

Roycroft put his eye to the parlour window, and on seeing Harding face down in the dirt, wiped the sweat from his brow. He hurried to his drinks cabinet and, dispensing with the fancy crystal glass that he normally used, the banker grabbed a bottle of whiskey and slugged like any saloon drunk, until the liquid dribbled down his chin. It took a long time, even with a second helping of whiskey, to settle his nerves down.

Belle Black was cringing under her father's thunder-laden scowl.

'He was just about to give me the name of the man who paid him to waylay me, Belle.'

Contritely, Belle apologized.

'Sorry, Pa. But from where I stood, it looked like Harding was getting ready to take you with him to Hades!'

Two of the fighting men from the Jug o' Grog, whose heads the sheriff had often banged together, had grabbed hold of Abe Black to support him, as he hobbled about, using a broom handle delivered to him by the Widow Collins as a crutch.

'I seen Roycroft headed into that alley, just afore the bust-up in the Jug o' Grog got goin', Marshal,' a sandy-haired horse-wrangler and sometimes horse-thief, if rumour was right, called Spider Rayburn, whispered in Abe Black's ear, and quickly added, 'And you didn't hear it from me. I got me a reputation to uphold.' He grinned.

Rayburn's information explained Luther Harding's flashing glance towards Jack Roycroft's house, just as he went down to Belle's rifle.

'Obliged, Spider,' Black thanked Rayburn.

'We'd best get you to Doc Forbes,' Rayburn's friend and partner in trouble-stirring said. 'That leg of yours is busted somethin' awful.' As they hoisted Black between them to carry him to Forbes's infirmary, Rayburn flashed a gal-winning smile Belle's way and complimented: 'Real fine shootin', Miss Belle.'

As they were going through the infirmary door, the focus of excitement and curiosity switched to the far end of town, to the two riders arriving.

'If my eyes ain't crooked from grog,' Spider Rayburn said. 'Buck Morgan's just landed on your doorstep, Marshal.'

7

The Big M boss rode straight down Main to the Forbes infirmary where he drew rein to address Abe Black who, at his request, and much to the annoyance of Doc Forbes, who wanted him inside, had had his helpers sit him in a rocker. Belle Black stood alongside her father. Luke Barrow brought his horse alongside his boss. The lines were clearly drawn.

'Howdy, Buck,' the marshal greeted the rancher. 'My condolences on the death of your boy.'

Bluntly, Morgan stated: 'I've come to hang the man who murdered my son, Marshal. I hope you're not going to stand between him and me.'

Barrow sniggered. 'Looks like he ain't goin' to be standin' any place for a long time, Mr Morgan.'

Morgan shot his foreman a visual reprimand.

66

'State your position, Abe?'

'My position is the one the law demands I take, Buck. Stoddard stands trial. He's got a right to his say, and the judgment of a properly constituted court of law.'

'Stoddard shot my son,' Morgan growled. 'Of that there seems no doubt.'

'I saw the smokin' gun in his mitt,' Barrow said. And addressing the crowd, 'A whole passel of us did. Ain't that so?' A sizeable part of the gathering murmured their agreement with Barrow. 'You saw it too,' he snarled at Black. 'So what're we waitin' for, Marshal? Let's get a rope and get Stoddard out here right now, I say.'

Abe Black said with quiet calmness, 'But none of us saw Stoddard shoot Randy Morgan.'

'It's as plain as daylight down a damn mine shaft what happened,' Barrow argued. 'That bastard Stoddard went to Linny Bates's room, as he's been doin' for quite a spell, found her pleasurin'

Randy and lost his head.'

'Though I didn't approve of my boy dallying with saloon trash,' Buck Morgan said, 'as Luke outlined it, I reckon is the way it happened, Abe. Stoddard's hankering for Linny Bates, as evidenced by his frequent visits to her, is common knowledge.'

'Things aren't always what they seem, Buck,' Abe Black said.

'Like I told ya, Mr Morgan,' Barrow growled, 'Black's been actin' as that cur's protector.'

'That's the way it looks, Marshal,' the rancher stated.

'Probably does at that,' Black said. 'But you've got to understand that, as the law in Willis Creek, it's my duty to see that Andy Stoddard gets a fair trial.'

'It's not fair to protect a killer from due justice,' Morgan flared.

'No, it isn't.' Abe Black's bleak grey eyes locked with the rancher's. 'But justice only becomes due, sir, after a judge and jury says so.'

68

Barrow uncoiled the lariat on his saddle horn and snorted. 'Let's go get that bastard and string him up right now, Mr Morgan!'

The crowd were of a mind with the Big M foreman. Buck Morgan wheeled his horse about and pointed the stallion towards the jail.

'It's what we've come to do, Luke. So, let's get it over with.'

The click of Abe Black's gun hammer brought a hush, and had Morgan's and Barrow's eyes flashing his way.

'I'll kill the first man who enters the jail,' Black threatened.

'You're bluffin',' Barrow snorted.

'Try me,' Black grunted.

Barrow's bravado slipped when faced with Abe Black's spiky ultimatum. He looked to Buck Morgan for guidance, but found his boss too busy trying to gauge the amount of gall in the marshal's response for himself.

'What's stopping you, Barrow?' Black growled.

The Big M ramrod sought backing

from the crowd which, to his annoyance, had suddenly dwindled. Those remaining returned neutral stares; at least those who weren't looking at their toecaps did.

'Mr Morgan?'

The rancher ignored his foreman's whining summons. He flung Abe Black a warning.

'I'm not leaving town until my son's killer swings, Marshal.'

Grittily uncompromising, Black replied.

'He will . . . But only if a jury says he's guilty.'

Morgan threatened: 'Jury or no jury. You can be certain that Stoddard will be rope-bait!'

Black warned: 'Any sign of jury-tampering or rigging and I'll have Stoddard's trial moved to another jurisdiction.'

Buck Morgan's retort was cut short as the marshal keeled over, the blood draining from his face to his toes.

'Get him inside fast,' Doc Forbes ordered a couple of men from the crowd, who turned their backs.

There were no volunteers. Any of a mind to help were warned off by Luke Barrow's angry scowl. On seeing Belle and the aged Sam Forbes frantically trying to haul the unconscious marshal into the infirmary, Buck Morgan ordered: 'Get the marshal inside!'

'But Mr Morgan, sir — '

The rancher turned on his foreman.

'The man needs help. It's the Christian thing to do.'

Belle Black raged at the cowards who now stepped forward, once Buck Morgan had given his approval.

'Get out of my sight you rats!'

With Abe Black inside the infirmary and settled, Luke Barrow strode back outside.

'There's nothin' stoppin' us slingin' a rope now fellas!' he declared.

Buck Morgan remained passive as Barrow led a ragbag lynch-mob to the jail. Ben Charles, who, moments before had joined Roycroft in his parlour, urged the banker:

'You've got to stop this, Jack. Talk to Morgan. Like I said, a lynching will bring a US marshal to town, and . . .'

'You wouldn't like that. Now would you, Ben,' Roycroft sneered. 'But you're right,' he conceded. 'We've all got skeletons in the closet that a US marshal might rattle.'

'Go talk to Buck Morgan.' The mortgage lender shoved the banker towards the parlour door, equal partners now after Roycroft's ready understanding of Charles's fears, and his own admission of skeletons in the closet. 'Tell him we've got things in hand. With Black out of the way and Barrow marshal, Stoddard is as good as hanged.'

'It would still be a lynching, Ben,' Roycroft murmured.

Charles smiled. 'Not with the plan I've got in mind.'

'And that would be?' the banker prodded.

'Wes Shine is a shyster. He can stand in, in the absence of a judge who's three weeks overdue as it is.' Charles smirked. 'It can reasonably be assumed that he's not going to show, can't it?'

Roycroft's look was one of open admiration. 'Well now, Ben,' he crooned. 'You're a real clever fella.'

The mortgage-lender laughed. 'Sure Stoddard's hanging will be a lynching. But it won't look like one. That way, no US marshal will come nose-poking, Jack.'

As events unfolded, Jack Roycroft's hurried visit to the street to talk with Buck Morgan was sidelined by Belle Black's intervention, as her Winchester cracked over Luke Barrow's head just as he led the bloodthirsty lynchers into the marshal's office. A large chunk of the overhang, ripped off by Belle's accurate shooting, struck Barrow on the side of the head and sent him reeling back into the street, where Belle's trio of follow-up bullets had the Big M foreman dancing, as her bullets bit at his boots.

'The lot of you back off!' Belle

warned, stepping into the street to confront the mob.

Buck Morgan's gun exploded to blast one of his own ranch hands as he slyly pulled iron to ambush Belle from the shadows.

'Thank you kindly, Mr Morgan.'

'Don't thank me, young lady,' he returned sourly. 'Could never abide bushwhackers. I might have to kill you myself, yet.'

'At least it'll be a fair fight, I reckon.'

'That it will be,' the rancher guaranteed her.

Barrow was confused by Buck Morgan's action. Had the boss gone loco? Skinny Wade had Belle Black in his sights.

Belle, keeping the mob under the threat of her Winchester, told Morgan; 'What my Pa said still stands. Andy Stoddard has a story to tell, and a right to tell it to a judge and jury.'

The Big M boss studied Belle for a long spell, during which her nerves jangled. If Buck Morgan chose to challenge her, there was no way that she could stop Stoddard being dragged from jail and strung up right there and then.

Relief turned Belle Black's legs to jelly when he said: 'Leave it be, Barrow!'

'Now it's my turn to thank you,' Belle said.

'Don't,' Morgan flung back. 'All you're getting is thinking time, young woman. I still aim to hang Stoddard for my boy's murder!'

Belle sighed wearily. 'That I can't let you do, Mr Morgan, sir.'

The rancher's ire leaped. 'Don't stand in my way again, Belle.'

Belle's sigh deepened. 'Don't see that there's much else I can do.'

Jack Roycroft stepped in. 'That killer's fate, Miss Black, will be up to the new marshal to decide.'

'New marshal?' Belle fumed. 'My pa is still marshal.'

Roycroft smiled patronizingly. 'In spirit, maybe. But he's busted up, Belle.

I reckon he won't be able to be a proper marshal this side of the election. And the town can't do without a marshal for that long. A town without a law enforcer would attract all sorts of no-goods. Willis Creek would be an open town in no time at all.'

The onlookers gave their full support to this assessment.

Roycroft went on: 'Your father is sure to have a bum leg after this, Belle. Which will prevent him doing his job in the way it should be done, anyway.'

Again, the onlookers agreed.

Ben Charles, who had followed the banker outside, prompted: 'Have you got a worthy someone in mind as a badge-toter, Jack?'

'In fact I do, Ben. I reckon Luke Barrow would be an able lawman.'

'Huh!' Barrow exclaimed. 'Me? A damn badge-toter?'

In a whispered aside, Roycroft said to Buck Morgan: 'Back my proposal and Stoddard is ropebait, Buck.'

Morgan did. 'I'll miss you as my foreman, Luke,' he said. 'But the town's needs are greater now than mine. I want you to stand in for Abe Black. When he's on his feet again, you can come straight back to being the Big M's ramrod, as if nothing changed.'

'But, Mr Morgan, sir,' Barrow griped.

Morgan threw in a sweetener. 'I'll continue to pay you, Luke.'

'You will?' Barrow asked, his jaw hitting his chest. Greed took over. 'Do I get the marshal's shekels as well?'

'You will,' Roycroft confirmed.

'Gosh.' He laughed. 'Then I'm your man, Mr Roycroft.'

Belle Black had a dilemma that needed solving fast. If Roycroft succeeded in planting Luke Barrow in the marshal's chair, Andy Stoddard wouldn't stand a chance of having his day in court. There was nothing for it but to lie!

'Hold up there,' she said.

All eyes turned Belle Black's way.

Jack Roycroft, amused, asked indulgently, 'What is it now Belle?'

'Barrow can't be the marshal.'

Her announcement brought new zest to the proceedings.

'Yeah,' Barrow griped. 'Who says?'

'That, Miss Black,' the banker said silkily, 'is a very good question.'

'I do,' Belle returned uncompromisingly. 'Because, according to town law, when the marshal is indisposed or dies his deputy takes over for the remainder of the marshal's tenure to the next election. Pa made me his deputy.'

'You?' Jack Roycroft yelped.

'Me!' Belle flung back.

Her defiant gaze went Wes Shine's way. He had just joined Ben Charles on the boardwalk outside Roycroft's house to lend his weight to Roycroft's skulduggery.

'Isn't that the town law, Mr Shine?'

Shine, wilting under his partners' stares, cringed.

'Isn't it?' Belle Black insisted.

'Guess so,' Shine admitted.

'Have you got rocks in your head?' Charles growled in an angry aside to Shine. 'What you just said rules Barrow out.'

Shine whined. 'It's the town law, Ben. There's nothing I can do.'

'That settles that,' Belle told Roycroft. 'I'm now marshal of Willis Creek.'

'A petticoat marshal?' Barrow hollered.

Roycroft snarled. 'I don't know of any town who's got a female law officer.'

'We'll be the laughing stock of the damn West, that's what we'll be!' Buck Morgan said.

'Don't fret, Buck,' the banker said. 'We'll soon get this sorted out.'

Belle Black squared up to Roycroft. 'It's sorted. The rules don't say that a woman can't be marshal.'

'That's because no one ever thought it would happen,' Roycroft bellowed.

'Well it has.' Belle faced the crowd. 'You'll have a chance to vote me out of office come election time. But until then, I run the law in this town. So go on home. There's going to be no lynching.'

Barrow, seething at having being denied a double salary, angrily stepped forward to face down the new marshal, his hand hovering over the Colt on his right hip.

'These others can accept your lip if they want, Belle Black. But I won't!'

Belle ducked low as Barrow's gun cleared leather and she came up like a top, on the ball of one foot, Winchester raised and spitting. The Big M foreman's hat spun into the air, and while it was there Belle placed another bullet in its crown to whip it further along Main. Stunned, Barrow stood stock-still as Belle's rifle came level with his belly.

'Like I said. Go on home.'

Belle Black's prowess with a gun came as a thunderbolt surprise to everyone. In the West, women sewed and baked and kept house; gun-slickness was not a common talent amongst womenfolk.

The crowd began to drift away, muttering. Belle Black gave the same message to Buck Morgan as Abe had. There would be no illegal hangings in Willis Creek, while a Black sported the marshal's badge.

She told Morgan. 'You might as well go on home, too, Mr Morgan. I'll let you know when the judge arrives.'

Thwarted, Morgan raged.

'This town's got one day to put Andy Stoddard's neck in a noose. If you don't, I'll ruin this town and everyone in it!' He wheeled his stallion about, sideswiping Roycroft, sending him sprawling in the dirt. 'I don't know what your plans are, mister,' he grated. 'But your next one better work!'

He rode on a few paces before delivering to Roycroft a mind-numbing ultimatum.

'String Stoddard up, or I'll take out every cent I have in your vault. I do that and your bank will belly up, Roycroft. And with it this town.'

Although it was a mild night, Jack

Roycroft had the chill of snow in his bones. The last thing he could deal with was an audit of bank records that had too many unexplained and unexplainable holes in them. There was no way he could cover the twenty thousand dollars he had stolen from Buck Morgan to invest in East Coast businesses which went bust. He had to get Stoddard on the end of a rope, fast, to keep his embezzlement secret until he could make up the loss to bank funds, or run.

There was also another and even more compelling reason to have Andy Stoddard hanged, and the book closed on Randy Morgan's murder. Trials were unpredictable things, often opening a can of worms. There was always the danger that the name of Linny Bates's real killer would somehow come to light, and he wouldn't at all like to hear it mentioned.

Because that name was his.

8

Belle Black went back inside Doc Forbes' infirmary to check on her father. He was out cold, sweating profusely and tossing about.

'It's a nasty wound,' Forbes told her. 'He won't die, if I can keep infection at bay, Belle. But he sure as hell won't win any dancing prizes when he's on his feet again. That leg of his will be there, hopefully, but it will be ramrod-straight and as heavy as lead, I reckon.'

Forbes took Belle by the shoulders.

'Abe won't be much use as a marshal with a bum leg, Belle. In fact it would be downright dangerous for him to continue to wear a badge.' He turned her towards the infirmary door. 'Now shoo, gal. It isn't going to be a pretty sight seeing me trying to get that leg straightened. I don't want any hysterics or fainting while I'm doing it. You go and wait in the marshal's office, and I'll come see you when it's over.'

Belle thanked Forbes and left with a lead-heavy heart. On going outside, a flaring match across the street caught her attention. Luke Barrow's meanly drawn features were lit by its yellow glow. Two other men, one a Big M hand, Ace Mooney, the other a town hooligan, formed a trio. The men's insolent posture gave warning of their hell-bent prodding for trouble. It surprised and disappointed Belle to see Mooney in such low dregs company. She had often exchanged greetings and banter with him on his visits to town. Last spring he had saved her from drowning in a swollen creek as she foolishly tried to cross it when the creek was flooded by melting snow. She had formed the opinion that he was a cut above most of the other Big M rannies. Looked like she was wrong.

Belle ignored the trouble-seeking trio, and walked on.

'Never seen a marshal walk so purty

afore, Luke,' Brad Dannon the town hooligan sniggered.

'She can take me to jail anytime she likes.' Ace Mooney grinned

'Now fellas,' Luke Barrow chastised his pards in a school master's tone, 'show some respect for our new marshal.'

Belle, not given to patience, reluctantly continued on her way, galled to have to keep her cork in, figuring that to round on the prodding trio would only add to their pleasure and stoke their jibing.

'Old Abe's got a real looker in that gal,' Dannon said. 'Ya know, when the marshal gets his *leg* under him again,' Barrow and the other Big M man leaned on each other laughing, 'I might just tell him that I'd be prepared to take Belle off his hands.'

Belle's cork blew and she swung around, madder than a stepped-on rattler. Dannon instantly stepped aside from Barrow and his Big M cohort to challenge: 'You want something,

Marshal?' His hip-jutting stance made the licentious meaning of his question clear.

Brad Dannon had been on the wrong side of Abe Black more times than most town hooligans, and had spent a lot of bone-sore hours in the town jail, after ending up on the receiving end of the marshal's fists. So, getting a chance to even the score some with a Black, even a woman, was one he was eager to take. He fancied himself as a budding gunfighter. He had the gun-slickness, but not the brains, to live long in that profession.

Belle Black, though a straight shooter, was not Dannon's equal. She had got the drop on Barrow earlier, but she knew that surprise could only work in her favour once. Barrow or Dannon would outdraw her any time of their choosing. Maybe Mooney, too. Though she doubted his gun prowess, and he'd never shown any kinship with an iron.

Barrow stepped up alongside Dannon. Ace Mooney hesitated, but could not withstand Barrow's and Dannon's scornful glances. He, too, stepped forward.

Coming on to the hotel veranda, Buck Morgan broke the impasse.

'Go on home, fellas. Barrow, you bed down in the livery. Mooney head back to the Big M.'

'I don't have to take no orders from you, Morgan,' Brad Dannon griped.

Luke Barrow's fist lashed out to send the townie sprawling on the ground.

'You don't give no lip to Mr Morgan, you hear.'

Brad Dannon's eyes glittered like Christmas tinsel with anger. He sprang up, his hand diving for iron.

'Hold it!' Belle Black commanded. She was still holding the Winchester she'd been toting since dropping Luther Harding and now she trained it on Dannon.

'This is 'tween Dannon and me!' Barrow snarled, and took up a duellist's stance.

'If you boys have a gripe to fix, do it

outside town,' Belle grated.

'Let the cur be, Barrow,' Buck Morgan ordered.

Reluctantly forcing his ire down, Barrow replied: 'As you want, Mr Morgan.'

'You're a real ass-kisser, ain't ya, Barrow.' Dannon taunted the Big M foreman.

'We'll fix this another time,' Barrow flung back.

'You bet,' snarled Willis Creek's prime hooligan.

The trio stalked off, Barrow to the livery, Dannon to the Jug o' Grog, Ace Mooney to his horse, each man flashing their hatred Belle Black's way. Before he hit leather, Mooney paused to address Belle in a spite-filled tone.

'You and your pa shouldn't be protecting Linny Bates's killer, Belle.' His voice cracked with emotion. 'Linny was OK. Not like other saloon women.'

Belle headed back to the law office, then changed her mind and went back to the infirmary to talk to Sam Forbes.

The doc had enough on his hands, but she needed help.

'You want me to what?' Forbes exploded, on hearing the new marshal's proposal.

'I need someone to guard Andy Stoddard, Doc, while I ride over to Clancyville to seek Marshal Cade's help. Pa was right. I'm way out of my depth and sinking fast.'

'I'm a doctor, Belle. I've never fired a shot in anger. Besides, I've got patients to tend to.'

'Doc Higgins will help out, I'm sure.'

'Higgins? He's a damn horse-doctor, Belle!'

'He did OK with two-legged critters when you were down with fever last winter.'

Forbes searched for a reasonable counter to Belle's argument, but could not find one. He conceded: 'I guess the mean old cuss did at that.'

Belle pleaded: 'If I don't get help, I reckon sooner or later a lynch mob will haul Stoddard out. And if I leave and have no one to mind the office, how long do you think it'll be before my prisoner is swinging in the breeze?'

Forbes dithered. Belle nibbled at his conscience.

'I'll ride, first light. I'm figuring on a couple of hours there and a couple more back. With any luck, I'll be back before anyone even knows I'm gone.'

Sam Forbes did some more dithering. Belle did some more chipping.

'You're a fair man,' Belle said, which he was. 'You don't want lynch law in your town no more than my pa and me do.'

'Damn your eyes, Belle Black,' Forbes groaned, 'you know I don't.' He marched back to where Abe Black lay restlessly. 'You go round up Dan Higgins. You need rest. I'll be along shortly. Now get out. I've got doctoring to do.'

★   ★   ★

In Jack Roycroft's parlour, his arguments for hanging-tree justice had lost their persuasiveness and appeal. Wes Shine, in the banker's opinion always the weak link, was now for letting events take their legal course, 'Now that we haven't delivered Randy Morgan's killer to his father when he rode in, as we planned,' he reasoned.

Ben Charles, too, fearful of the brewing ruckus attracting the attention of a US marshal, was against a lynching, not on principle, but from a self-preservation stance.

'Have you gone yellow on me too, Frank?' Roycroft quizzed the mercantile store-owner.

Burton's eyes slid away from the banker's. 'Seems to me that Buck Morgan might settle for a trial, Jack, if it was fast. Buck surely hasn't the poison to go up against a woman, I reckon. He slapped Barrow down fast enough when he wanted to.'

'Yeah,' Charles enthused, eager to avoid the kind of trouble that would attract a high-calibre lawman to town, 'a fast trial is the answer.' He went on to explain the plan he'd earlier outlined to Roycroft, about having Wes Shine as the judge and Barrow as the marshal.

Roycroft dampened Shine's and Burton's enthusiasm for Ben Charles's scheme.

'Making room for Barrow might not be easy. The town mightn't stand for a second Black put in the infirmary.'

'Not in the same way that Belle's pa was,' Charles agreed. 'But I'm sure an accident could be arranged.'

'Not too serious an accident,' Burton fretted. 'Belle is a woman, after all.'

Roycroft went along with the group's enthusiasm for the mortgage lender's plan, but knew that he didn't have the kind of time that would be needed to pull the threads of Ben Charles's scheme together. As he'd threatened, any time at all Buck Morgan could be on the bank's doorstep to close his account. If he did, it would leave precious little of the townsfolk's savings. The hole in Buck Morgan's assets brought about by his unwise investments, would have to be filled with those savings. That would leave the bank almost skint. And his hide up for whipping. Then there were his partners in scheming, too. Burton, Charles and Shine had substantial accounts at the bank. At least they thought they had . . .

The banker ran a finger inside a collar that was suddenly two sizes too small. The trio were looking at him with shrewd, curious eyes. Seeing Jack Roycroft flustered was something they'd never witnessed before.

Damn! Did he have to talk in his sleep? It had been a facet of his make-up that had begun in childhood and continued still. It was why he had remained a bachelor. He had done too many dirty deals and swindles to share a bed, not knowing what secrets his loose mouth might give away. Like the secret Linny Bates had got hold of. Why had he drunk so much and fallen asleep that night a week ago, when she had called to pleasure him. Then, a week later, just when he'd thought he'd held his tongue and was safe, having worked out her plan of ensnarement, Linny called at the bank. He shuddered now on recalling that visit.

'Why, hello there, Jack,' she had purred, saucily.

He knew right off that he was in trouble. He had never permitted her to call him by his first name. She was a saloon whore. Trash. He burned inside at the familiarity, but he smiled.

'Hello, Linny. What can I do for you?' He'd slipped out of his chair to pull down the blind, and then crossed to the door to lock it. 'We wouldn't want to be disturbed.'

The bed-hopping tramp had laughed.

'You don't want no one to know that I'm here, do you now, *Jack*,' she laughed. 'I mean saloon whores don't have need to call on bankers during business hours.' She'd taunted him.

'Don't worry, Jack. I came in the side door from the alley. No one saw me.'

He had come straight to the point.

'What do you want, Linny?'

'Well, now,' she'd ambled around the office as if she'd owned it, poking where she felt like poking. 'No need to rush, is there, Jack?'

Roycroft had licked parched lips. 'A hundred dollars, maybe? To buy some fancy new dresses.'

Linny Bates's scoffing laughter still rang in his ears.

'You were real talkative the other night, Jack.' She'd helped herself to his best French brandy, given only to clients of Buck Morgan's standing. She had let the liquid wash about her mouth, making nauseating sucking sounds, leaving rouged lip-stains on the fine crystal glass. 'I could get real used to this, after years of supping rot-gut.' She had poured a drink for him, laughing lazily as she poured. 'You'd best have some, too. Because there ain't goin' to be much of this fine brew for you once Buck Morgan finds out that you've been rifling the stash he gave you to hold for him. Buck, when riled good, can be meaner than his son Randy, and that's an awful lot of meaness, Jack.'

'Five hundred,' he had sweated.

'No.'

'A thousand,' he'd gasped.

'Maybe. But, you know. I was figuring that as your wife — '

'My wife?'

Even now, a week later, his head reeled.

'Are you sayin' that I'm not good enough to share your bed on a permanent basis, Mr High and Mighty Roycroft?' Linny Bates had flared.

'You wouldn't be happy as my wife, Linny,' he'd chuckled nervously. 'I'm bachelor goods. I'm not fit to be a husband. I haven't got the qualifications!'

'What's to it?' Linny cackled. 'All you'd have to do is dress me in fine clothes, walk me on your arm around town, and take me to swill that expensive Italian wine you and your swanky friends guzzle at them dinner parties!'

Roycroft recalled having to grab the edge of his desk to support himself, such was the terrible shock that he had suffered. Somehow, he had managed to smile and make Linny Bates believe that there might be a chance he'd meet her outrageous proposition.

'Why, you know, Linny . . . ' he'd circled her, 'having you in my bed permanently might not be such a bad idea after all!'

'Why pay when you can have it free, right Jack?'

Roycroft cringed even now as her lewd, vulgar laughter echoed in his ears.

'How about you dropping by tonight,' he'd managed to say. He had bent down to kiss her rouged cheek, and put a playful arm around her waist. 'We can make our plans then.'

When she left, he had at once made his plans to sneak up the outside stairs of the Jug o' Grog and hide in the giant wardrobe in Linny's room to lay wait in ambush. She never entertained before ten o'clock, spending the earlier part of the night getting the Jug o' Grog's imbibers to buy Sullivan's cheap whiskey, a special brand of loco juice that he brewed in his own still in the mountains east of town, from a recipe that he'd brought over from Ireland.

Linny was a creature of habit and always came to her room before she entertained her first client of the night, to put on fresh lip-rouge and dab on the cheap scent she stank of. It was then that Roycroft had planned to kill her. With a smidgen of luck, he'd be out of her room, through the window at the end of the hall, and back down the outside stairs to the dark alley in seconds.

But bad luck had dogged him. Linny changed her habitual time in the Jug o' Grog and arrived with Randy Morgan in tow. Roycroft, with his eye to a crack in the panel of the wardrobe door, through which he could watch, hoped that he could safely hole up in the wardrobe. Randy had the reputation of being a buck, with boundless energy. Linny could open the wardrobe at any second. Different men liked different things, and the rancher's son might have a preference for Linny to wear some naughty garment, of which there was a variety, many of which he himself recognized.

The scene replayed in Roycroft's mind, as clearly as if he were there at that moment. Randy Morgan licked his fingers and put them on the oil-lamp wick to quench its flame, plunging the room into darkness. He dragged Linny on to the bed and began to fool around. Just then the door opened and Stoddard stepped into the room. Interrupted in taking his pleasure, Randy Morgan reared up and grabbed his pistol which he had placed on a bedside locker, cutting loose at Stoddard in a rage. Stoddard ducked and fell over. Linny Bates began screaming and pulling Morgan back on to the bed, as he drunkenly peered into the dark to end what he'd started.

Taking advantage of the chaos in the room, the banker had covered his head with one of Linny's black shoulder shawls that she favoured, then had sprung from the wardrobe, grabbed the gun that Linny was tussling with Morgan for control of, whacked Stoddard across the skull as he got from the floor to help Linny, and then had laid lead in both Randy Morgan and Linny Bates. He had planned to strangle Linny, and had some scary moments as he ran along the hall to escape through the window into the night, chased by the sound of gunfire. But his nerve had held long enough to put the six-gun in the dazed Andy Stoddard's hand. Luckily, a kerfuffle in the saloon had caused confusion that served him well.

When he reached the edge of the alley, Abe Black was already bursting through the saloon's batwings, and an excited and curious crowd were milling about. It was as easy as stealing candy from a blind man to slip quietly away, as all eyes were on the Jug o' Grog.

'You're all in a lather, Jack.'

Ben Charles's observation prised Roycroft loose from his reverie. The banker was quick to react to explain his profuse perspiration.

'I think I'm coming down with something. Feel all feverish.'

Frank Burton, who was standing close to the banker, immediately distanced himself.

'There was fever in that wagon train that skirted town last week.'

Roycroft saw the opportunity to rid himself of his partners. He needed time to think clearly. He obliged with a rasping cough and staggered weakly.

Ben Charles was first to the door, promising: 'I'll look in later, Jack.'

'Me too,' Frank Burton added, hot on the mortgage-lender's heels.

Wes Shine grabbed the chance to be first out of the room as Charles and Burton made their excuses.

★ ★ ★

'Every word on that page is gospel-true, Miss Belle,' Andy Stoddard assured Belle, as she checked the facts of his statement to her father. Belle shook her head.

'You'll have a hard time making anyone believe it.'

'That's the way with the truth sometimes. It's so strange that it reads like lies.'

'Only me, Belle,' Doc Forbes called as he entered the outer office. He had known one or two men who had ended up on his operating table from time to time because they hadn't announced themselves when folk were jittery.

'Hello, Doc,' Belle greeted wearily, as she came through the connecting door from the office to the cells. 'How's Pa?'

'Right now he looks a whole lot better than you,' Forbes said. 'You need to shut those pretty hazel eyes of yours. Go home, Belle. Get some rest, or you'll be joining your father in the infirmary,' He chuckled. 'And I damn well don't want two mule-headed patients at the same time.'

Forbes went to the gun cabinet, took out a shotgun, broke it, inserted two cartridges, sat in the marshal's chair with the gun across his lap, patted the Greener and declared: 'The first unfriendly cur that pokes his head round that door will go away shot full of pellets!'

He laughed uproariously.

'Which he'll have to pick out of his butt himself, seeing that I'm the only doc for over thirty miles of a round trip.'

Belle, though worried about railroading Abe Black's old friend into helping out, laughed along with him.

'You're sure you'll be OK, Doc?'

'I'm sure, Belle. I might look sixty, but I think thirty. Now git!' Belle left the law office.

The night had an eerie, expectant stillness to it — the kind of night that at any second could erupt in violence. The saloons had closed early on Belle's orders, Joseph Sullivan co-operating right off, while the owners of the other two watering-holes had to be persuaded by the threat of stiff fines under town law for refusing a legitimate order of the town marshal. No one knew, of course, though she suspected that the wily Sam Forbes might, that she was not the legitimate marshal of Willis Creek. Belle's earlier lie about her father having made her his deputy, and consequently marshal in his absence, did not trouble her one jot. It was a toss-up between her untruth and Luke Barrow's wearing a star. In Belle's book, she did not have much option but to lie.

As she walked to her house at the south end of Main, the quieter side of town, which would probably end up the swankiest as the town developed into a city, as everyone hoped it would, Belle checked each moving shadow. She'd have given a lot for a full moon, instead of the heavy rain-clouds that had swept in an hour before. Though she walked with an arrogant swagger, her heart raced, fearing that at any second one of the shadows would materialize, sporting a pistol.

There wasn't much point in her going home anyway, she wasn't going to sleep, but it would please Doc Forbes to think that she was heeding his advice. On her way, she called at the infirmary.

'I gave your pa a sleeping potion, Belle.' Dan Higgins laughed. 'The same potion I gave Larry Fleming over at the livery to knock out a hurting horse.' Belle's face lit with alarm. 'No need to fret, Belle,' Higgins assured her. 'The potion for a stallion and your pa would be about the same, I reckon.' He chuckled on seeing Belle's face pale. 'Only kidding. You come by tomorrow. Abe will be all bushy-tailed by then!'

Belle continued on home. Just as she approached the house, she poked her toe on a stone and stumbled. At that second a gun cracked and the breeze of a bullet ruffled her fringe, and continued on to shatter the parlour window. She dived over the hedge and crouched low. A second bullet came her way, but was just as harmless to life and limb as the first one. She heard the scuffle of running feet and caught sight of a scampering hunched figure at the far side of the street. Belle cut loose with a trio of shots, pleased to hear a howl from her attacker on the third. She cleared the hedge and gave chase, and the man ducked into an alley near the bank. Not having the guile of her father, she forgot, in her eagerness to catch her would-be assassin, to put an eye to the corner of the alley before bulling into it blind. A fist as solid as a smithy's anvil stopped her in her tracks and exploded rainbow colours in front of her eyes. She shot backwards in to the street and rolled like a wagon-wheel.

Sam Forbes was first to appear, filling the law office door, Greener pointing.

'Belle,' he called to the huddled

bundle in the middle of the street, 'is that you?' He called out to her attacker. 'Show yourself, whoever you are, and I'll dispatch you to the Devil where you rightly belong, you cur!'

Now the street was full of running people. The thing about a Western town and its divided loyalties was that all arguments were forgotten when a bushwhacker showed his hand. No one liked a bushwhacker.

Belle came round groggily, cradled in Forbes's arms.

'You OK, Belle?'

She rolled her head about. 'I guess so. Except that my face feels ten times its size.'

'Yeah,' Forbes confirmed, 'you're sure not going to look pretty for a spell.'

Recollection of why she was on the ground returned to Belle and she leaped up. She staggered about while hands tried to steady her. She angrily shook off her helpers and made tracks for the livery. When she arrived, Luke

Barrow curled up under the force of Belle Black's kick.

'What the hell was that for?' the Big M foreman reacted angrily.

Belle reached across him and pulled his Colt from its holster and sniffed at the barrel.

'Is this your only gun, Barrow?' she growled.

'You know I only pack one,' he replied angrily. 'What the hell did you just kick me for?'

'It seemed like a good idea at the time. Let me see you. Roll over.'

'What the hell for?'

'Just do it,' Belle grated.

There was no sign of blood on Barrow's clothes. Belle stormed off, the townfolk who had come to help her hot on her tail.

An old-timer explained to Barrow: 'Someone just tried to kill the marshal.'

Luke Barrow reacted spitefully. 'Yeah? Well, if you find him, bring him back here and I'll plug him m'self for missing that she-devil.'

Belle's next port of call was the Dannon house, where she hammered hard enough on the door to wake the dead in the town cemetery. Harry Dannon, a poor excuse for a man who spent most of his time supping on others' dregs in the town's saloons, opened the door, hitching up his trousers and complaining.

'You got no right to come chargin' in here, Belle Black.'

Belle ignored the rebuke and was heading up the stairs two at a time, her entourage piling in behind her. She kicked in Brad Dannon's bedroom door. Dannon sat up in bed bleary-eyed with sleep, naked as the day he came from his mother's womb, and not a scratch on him.

'Go back to sleep!' Belle barked, and slammed the door. On her way out she apologized to Harry Dannon. 'Sorry for the intrusion, Mr Dannon.'

The old-timer who had explained Belle Black's fury to Luke Barrow crowed excitedly: 'Where to now, Belle.'

'Home,' she told him. 'Where you should be, Ned Billings!'

She stalked off, checked in with Forbes in the jail, and then went on home, cursing and pondering on who, other than the pair she'd visited, would sling lead her way. She went straight to the kitchen. She lit the lamp. A pale, blood-drained face loomed up in its yellow glow.

'Sorry to scare you, Marshal,' Ace Mooney rasped breathlessly, grabbing the edge of the table to steady himself as he hauled himself out of the chair he was seated on. 'But you see, you and me got unfinished business.'

Belle looked down the barrel of his pistol as he brought the gun level with her face. His hand was shaking so bad that it could go off any second, as he toyed with its trigger. Belle noticed the splurge of red on his right side spreading wider by the second.

'Yeah, you got me good,' he sneered. 'But you're damn well goin' to be in hell before me, Belle Black.'

'You paid the price that a bush-whacker deserves to pay,' Belle grated. 'Why did you make this your fight anyway?'

His eyes filled with tears. 'I loved Linny Bates,' he declared. 'Loved her with all my heart. And that bastard Stoddard went and killed her. Sure I want him strung up. And he would've been if you hadn't saved his hide, you bitch!' The youngster's eyes lit with the devil's fire. 'Mebbe it ain't too late yet.' He shoved Belle ahead of him. 'Let's go hang him right now!'

With the Big M ranny's gun prodding her spine, Belle had no choice but to head for the jail. He drew her up short outside the law office.

'I knowed you got Doc Forbes in there with a shotgun. I seen him. Get him out here. Now!'

Belle ground her teeth.

'Doc. It's me. Belle . . . '

'I know who you are, Belle. But why aren't you coming on in?'

'I want you to come out, Doc.'

'Yeah?'

The kid raged. 'Get out here, you old fool. I gotta a gun in the marshal's back and so help me I'll pull the trigger if I don't see your craggy old face right now.'

The law office door opened slowly. Sam Forbes's shrewd eyes took in the no-win scene confronting him.

'Find a rope and get Stoddard out here,' Mooney ordered. 'We've got ourselves a neck-tie party to go to, Doc.'

9

Doc Forbes glanced helplessly at Belle Black.

'There's nothing you can do, Doc,' Belle said. 'Get Stoddard out here.'

'Sensible lady,' the Big M ranny scoffed.

'Damn, Belle,' Forbes swore frustratedly.

'Do as you're told, you old bastard!' Mooney yelled, with as much bluster as his weakened state would permit.

Fearful of Forbes bearing the brunt of Mooney's rage, Belle again instructed the town doctor to fetch Stoddard, though her eyes held another message. If he could read it, it told the medico to dally as long as he could, once he got inside. The wounded man was weakening fast from loss of blood and wouldn't be standing for much longer, Belle reckoned.

'No tricks,' the man warned the doc, as Forbes went back inside. 'Any sign of chicanery, and I'll blast the marshal.'

Belle hoped that Forbes's final glance her way, before entering the office, meant that he had correctly read her unspoken message. He was no fool. But with the threat of mayhem hanging over him, and his fear for Belle's safe passage through the crisis, the doc might not be as sharp as he normally was.

He was back out without delay. Or at least that was how it seemed to Belle. But under the threat of a gun time goes awry. So Forbes might have been longer than she thought. Her captor's fidgety foot-shuffling would suggest that he had. His angry accusation confirmed that he had.

'You took your damn time, Doc.'

'I'm not the marshal,' Forbes barked. 'I couldn't find the keys to Stoddard's cell.'

'Miss Belle,' Stoddard implored, eyes wild with fear, 'what's happenin'?'

Then, on seeing the Big M ranny's gun in her back, whined, 'They're goin' to hang me, ain't they?'

By now, alerted by the commotion, a sizeable crowd had gathered to witness the events outside the jail.

Stoddard accused Belle: 'Your pa told me that no one would get to hang me, until a judge said so. If he said so.'

The wounded man snarled.

'Well, things have changed some, Stoddard!' Spotting Luke Barrow, he called: 'Luke, bring that horse over here.'

Barrow eagerly unhitched the mare standing at the rail outside the Dancing Dove, Willis Creek's second of three saloons.

'Under that oak,' Mooney instructed, pointing to the sturdier of a pair in the town square; a tree known as the Hanging Tree, used before the town got civilized enough to build a gallows. Then, prodding Belle forward, he ordered Doc Forbes: 'Get Stoddard in the saddle!'

By now a blood-lust had gripped the onlookers, and Belle knew that she could expect no help from that quarter. If her captor would only put a couple of feet between them, she might get a chance to round on him, and get in a kick — the kind of pulverizing boot that the Changs called kung-fu, which they'd demonstrated and taught to Belle on her visits.

'You gotta stop this,' Andy Stoddard pleaded with Belle.

'With a gun in her back, there's nothing the marshal can do, son,' Sam Forbes said.

Barrow hurried forward to hoist Stoddard in the saddle. Belle's prisoner fought fiercely, but a clip on the side of the head from the Big M foreman's gun-butt took the fight out of him. As Barrow shoved him aboard the mare, Stoddard's senses were reeling.

Another man volunteered to sling the rope.

'That branch,' Ace Mooney instructed the man, indicating a branch half-way up the tree, 'that way he'll swing good!'

Spotting Buck Morgan observing impassively from the hotel veranda, Belle called out: 'Are you going to let this happen, Mr Morgan? If you do, you'll be as guilty of murder as every other man here!'

Barrow stalled his rabble-rousing to await his boss's decision.

'Whatcha waitin' for, Luke?' his Big M partner raged. 'Morgan's opinion don't matter a damn to me now. I've drawn my last dime this side of Hell!'

The crowd fell silent; they too were waiting on Buck Morgan's decision.

'Ain't no one goin' to help me hang this murderin' bastard?' Mooney screamed.

When the Big M boss turned and walked back into the hotel, it was the signal for the Devil to have his way. The noose was around Stoddard's neck when a shotgun boomed out. Most of the crowd flung themselves to the ground. Sam Forbes, blessedly, had the presence of mind to grab hold of the horse's reins to stop her bolting.

Joseph Sullivan, the giant-sized owner of the Jug o' Grog stepped out of the dark, shotgun ready to dispatch any dissenters or subdue any threat.

'Let it be, Barrow!' the rock-solid Irishman growled, as the Big M foreman's hand dived for his gun. 'And get that noose off Stoddard's neck.'

'Why're you savin' this cur's hide, Sullivan?' Ace Mooney challenged. 'Why should it bother you if Stoddard swings?'

Joeseph Sullivan stood square in front of the crowd.

'I had a brother once. His only crime was to steal a sack of potatoes to feed hungry mouths. He was strung up too, just like Stoddard nearly was just now. I don't hold with rough justice. And if someone don't get Stoddard off that horse and back to jail, this gun will start barking!'

A couple of men scrambled forward to take Stoddard off the horse.

'Leave him right where he is!'

Mooney shouted. Doc, let go of those reins.' Belle's ordeal was not over. Mooney put his gun-barrel to her head and ordered Sullivan: 'Shuck the blunderbuss, or so help me I'll drop the marshal.'

Sullivan was in a bind.

'Do it!' the Big M ranny shouted. 'And let go of those reins, Doc,' he ordered. 'I don't mind how many I take with me.'

Belle felt Mooney's grip suddenly slacken. Clearly the emotion of the last couple of minutes had drained him of what strength he had left. Grabbing her chance, she slipped out of his hold and, spinning around, leaped through the air, cutting loose with a hellish scream that would scare Satan witless, to land a pile-driving boot in the Big M man's jaw that whipped him off his feet and flung him backwards as if he were no heavier than a blade of grass. As he crashed to the ground, his gun went off and the horse bolted, leaving Andy Stoddard dangling. With lightning-quick reaction, Belle drew iron and split the hangman's rope with a bullet, sending her prisoner crashing to the ground. Joseph Sullivan rushed forward to loosen the rope around Stoddard's neck.

Seeing Stoddard breathing again, Belle turned her attention to Ace Mooney. His breathing was shallow and laboured. His eyes rolled up at her, tears flooding them.

'Sorry, Belle,' he groaned. 'Forgive me, huh?'

'I forgive you, Ace.' She summoned Forbes. 'You've got another patient, Doc.'

'Patient? Darn, he just tried to kill you, Belle.'

'That's something we'll have to chin-wag about when he's feeling up to it. Right now he needs doctoring.'

As Mooney was carried off to the infirmary, Forbes scratched his head and wondered:

'What the hell kind of fighting was that, Belle?'

'It's called kung-fu, Doc,' Belle informed him.

'Kung, what?'

'Chinese fighting skill,' Belle elaborated.

'Heck,' Sam Forbes grunted. 'It sure's got a sting in it, Belle.'

★   ★   ★

Jack Roycroft turned away from his parlour window, more worried than ever at what he'd seen. Sullivan's backing for Belle Black was a worry. But, he reckoned, Belle's feisty dispatch of the man who'd held her at gunpoint was probably even a greater cause for concern.

Belle Black was proving to be no pushover!

10

The Jug o' Grog owner volunteered to take over in the jail to allow Doc Forbes to minister to his new patient who, by God's will and Forbes's skill was still alive, though hovering on the brink of eternity. Forbes had removed Belle's bullet from his side and for now had stopped the bleeding, though that might not be the case for long.

'I've done all I can,' the medico told Belle when she called to enquire about Ace Mooney's health. 'I'll need the Almighty's continuing help.' Forbes screwed up his face. 'Why should you be worried about this murdering hog anyway? He tried to kill you, Belle.'

It was a very good question, for which Belle had no answer for herself or Sam Forbes!

'He was in love with Linny Bates. He saw me as her killer's protector, Doc. A broken heart can make a body very bitter, and a lot loco.'

Belle's mind went back to Ike Westcoff, a charming drifter who had ambitions to be a gunfighter, who had blown into town three years before to capture her heart. Blind as love can make a woman or man, she could see no wrong in him, seeing his arrogant swagger and his mean nature as the mark of a man, instead of the posturing of a coward. Her father had tried to talk sense to her, but she was so feverish for Westcoff that reason had deserted her, and she resented parental interference, as she saw it then. When her father ran the would-be gunslinger out of Willis Creek, she ran after him. A week later, the blinkers of love were lifted from her eyes in the rawest fashion when Westcoff callously gunned down a half-blind old-timer who made the mistake of falling over his outstretched legs on a saloon porch over in Oakville, and spilled flour on his new-pin trousers. Up to that point, much like

Ace Mooney would kill for Linny Bates, she also might have killed for Ike Westcoff. Having been smitten and broken-hearted, Belle Black could understand Ace Mooney's pain and his remedy for it, too. She smiled now on recalling Abe Black's dry-as-desert comment when she arrived back home, downhearted, downtrodden and hurting.

'I reckon the other prodigal's absence was a mite longer, Belle!' Then he hugged her and cried. 'But your return is sure as hell every bit as sweet!'

'Belle . . . ' Her father's holler from the next room broke her reverie. 'You get in here. We've got some talking to do, gal.'

She found her father sitting up in bed, angry as a spooked rattler, and ranting:

'What the devil do you think you're playing at, Belle?'

'Settle down, Abe,' Doc Forbes advised. 'Exploding blood-vessels aren't going to help any.'

'I guess your tetchiness is down to me being marshal,' Belle said.

'You're a woman,' Abe Black growled, 'though I must admit that sometimes you act more in keeping with trousers instead of a petticoat!' His anger turned to raw concern. 'But toting a star is going too far, Belle.' Then anger returned to his grey eyes. 'Do you think the scum trying to put a noose around Andy Stoddard's neck are going to shoot around you because you wear petticoats?'

'Well, Pa,' Belle groaned, slapping a hand to jeans-clad thigh, I haven't worn a petticoat since I was twelve years old.'

'Don't trade words with me, Belle,' Abe Black grated. 'You know what I mean.' His mood took on a few more degrees of heat. 'Besides, you can't be marshal!'

Belle urgently shushed her father. 'Town law says I can, if I was your deputy, Pa.'

'Well, you're not!'

Belle slapped a hand over her father's

mouth. 'No one knew that. Now I reckon they know in Texas!' Frustrated with her father's barracking, Belle grittily asked: 'Would you prefer to see Luke Barrow wearing the marshal's badge?'

'Barrow?' he exclaimed. 'That dog's turd a marshal?'

'Well,' Belle crowed, 'it was him or me. So I lied, and told them that you had made me your deputy and, being your deputy, under town law, I automatically succeeded to the marshal's office while you were incapacitated. If Barrow had got a star, how long do you think it would take him to string Stoddard up?'

Finding new rage, Abe demanded: 'Who the hell wanted Barrow as marshal, Belle?'

'Well, he seemed to be a popular choice, Pa. But the prime mover behind his nomination was Jack Roycroft.'

'Roycroft, huh?' Black said thoughtfully. He recalled the way Luther Harding's eyes had drifted to Roycroft's house before he died, and he figured that his gesture had spoken louder than any words. If he'd read Harding's eyes correctly, it meant that it was the banker who had put those dollars in his hand to bushwhack him.

Why?

He could understand Roycroft and his cronies wanting to kowtow to Buck Morgan to protect their pockets, by delivering swift justice to Randy Morgan's supposed killer. He also reckoned that the town's need to have Stoddard at the end of a rope was primarily motivated by the same reasoning. If Buck Morgan obtained the goods and services for the mighty Big M elsewhere, a lot of folk would be the poorer for it. But, worthy as Roycroft's and his cronies' motivation was, and shaky as their nerves might be, bushwhacking the marshal to replace him with a lawman more amenable to stretching Stoddard's neck seemed a loco thing to do. Was his opposition to Stoddard's lynching reason and motive enough to warrant the banker hiring Luther Harding's services? Or was there another reason? Maybe a reason that was even more important to Jack Roycroft than getting in Buck Morgan's good books? So, Abe pondered, what was Roycroft's *real* reason and urgency to get Stoddard's neck in a noose?

He shared his thoughts with Belle.

'I've got to get out of here,' he said.

'You stay right where you are, Abe Black,' Belle commanded. 'Right where Doc Forbes can keep an eye on that shot-up leg of yours!'

Appearing in the doorway, Forbes rebuked the marshal.

'Belle's right, Abe. If you're not really careful, you could be left with one pin for the New Year's dance.' He chuckled. 'Come to think of it, you'd probably still dance as well.'

'I can't keep my butt in this bed while Belle's hide is at risk, Doc,' Black growled.

'Well, now,' the medico opined, 'I've

seen Belle in action, Abe, and I for one would not unduly rile her. And I don't think anyone else will, outside that dunderhead Barrow maybe, who I'm sure Belle will subdue easily enough,' he confided to Black. 'That gal's got more spit than most men I've seen come down the track,' he enthused. 'You should have seen her flying boots, Abe?'

'Flying boots?' Black enquired.

'Kung-fu,' Belle replied. In explanation to her father's puzzlement she added: 'It's a special kind of Chinese fighting that the Changs taught me. Came in mighty handy too, Pa.'

Forbes contributed: 'The darnedest thing I ever did see, Abe. Belle just took off like a buzzing bee and hung up there in mid-air, before twisting like a snake to land a boot in Ace Mooney's jaw that pulverized him.'

'I'm still getting out of this bed,' Abe Black pronounced.

'Let him be,' Forbes told Belle as she tried to hold him down.

'Let him be, Doc?' she questioned hotly.

'Let him be, Belle,' he re-emphasized.

'You're talking sense at last, you old coot,' Black chided Forbes.

'Now,' the doctor said a moment later, as Abe Black lay on the floor, howling, his leg as useless as cotton-wool, 'help me get him back in bed, Belle!'

When her father was settled back in bed, Belle told him: 'I'm riding over to Clancyville to get help from Marshal Cade, Pa. He's got a pair of deputies. I figure he can let me have the services of one until this brouhaha blows over. While I'm gone, Joseph Sullivan will stand watch over Stoddard.'

'Good idea,' Abe Black endorsed, his eyes shut tight with the ferocity of his pain. Concerned, Belle looked to Forbes.

'He'll be fine,' the medico, confirmed. 'If he acts sensibly, that is!'

On leaving the infirmary, Belle headed straight for her horse and cut a trail out of town for Clancyville. It was barely after daybreak, but Jack Roycroft, sleep impossible for him, saw her leave, and reckoned her destination to be Clancyville and not Oakville — the marshal there, not being the kind of sterling lawman that Ben Cade over in Clancyville was, would be unsympathetic to Belle Black's plight.

The banker hurried from the house to the livery to seek out Luke Barrow.

'What the dev . . . ?' Barrow groused as Roycroft shook him awake. 'Can't a fella get a wink of shut-eye in this burg!' The Big M foreman itched from his straw bed. Surlily, he asked, 'What d'ya want, Roycroft?'

'The same as you, Barrow. Andy Stoddard swinging!'

'You woke me to tell me that?' Barrow growled.

'I woke you up to tell you that Belle Black has left town as if the Devil himself was on her tail.' Barrow came instantly alert. Roycroft continued. 'I reckon, she's gone to get help from Ben

Cade over in Clancyville.'

'You think we should haul Stoddard out now and string him up?'

'If you want to risk a belly full of buckshot from that lunatic Irishman, Sullivan, who's standing guard while Belle is beating a track for Clancyville!'

'But if she's gone for help, we ain't got time to dally. There's a deputy over in Clancyville, name of Jed Wood, fast as a spit with an iron and as tough as railroad track, too.'

'Maybe you should head over Clancyville way yourself, Barrow?' the banker slyly suggested. His conniving tone slid down a notch. 'And maybe you could take a travelling companion or two along for company?'

Barrow, about as bright as a quenched oil-lamp, took some time to work out the intricacies of the banker's suggestion. When the penny finally dropped, the Big M foreman smiled broadly.

'You know, Mr Roycroft, come to

think of it, I ain't been there in a long while.'

Roycroft slipped a thick roll of dollar bills into Barrow's hand. 'You make sure you and your friends enjoy your trip, Luke!'

Barrow flicked the bills between his fingers, his glowing eyes expressing his satisfaction. 'I surely will, Mr Roycroft, sir. But you be sure to wait till I get back for that neck-tie party, you hear. I wouldn't wanna miss a hangin'.'

'You'll be slinging the rope, Luke,' Roycroft promised.

11

Luke Barrow skimmed off half of his ill-gotten gains and then grandiosely split the remainder, which he put forward as the total poke, with his two cronies, Brad Dannon and Spitter Doyle (so called because of his prowess for aiming accurately into the Jug o' Grog's spittoons from twenty paces) three ways. Heeding Roycroft's advice, they walked their horses to the edge of town to avoid drawing attention to themselves by riding out helter-skelter. The early morning town was still silent, and the hoofs of three horses leaving at a gallop would be sure to earn attention and be remarked upon later, when the news of Belle Black's demise reached Willis Creek.

Once outside town, Barrow spurred his horse and set a breakneck pace for the others to follow. Belle Black had a good half-hour start on them, and the closer she got to Clancyville the riskier it would be to kill her. Ben Cade, Clancyville's marshal, worked his deputies hard, sending them out daily to reconnoitre the countryside around the town, to watch for any trouble that might be riding their way.

Barrow had an intimate knowledge of the terrain. Having spent most of ten years ramrodding for the Big M, he had seen country and trails that less inquisitive folk had never set hoof or foot on. He had one such trail in mind now. It would cut a good twenty minutes off the more direct route to Clancyville that Belle Black would have taken, and with a little more push and a smidgen of luck, he'd reach the rocky pass that Belle Black would have to ride through to reach Clancyville, ahead of the marshal. The narrow confines of the pass would make her a sitting target for his gun.

★　★　★

135

Belle Black rode her horse steadily, resisting the temptation to ride full out. The trail to Clancyville had trying stretches along its length that a tired horse could fold up on. The need for a steady pace clashed with her desire not to be away from Willis Creek for too long. Joseph Sullivan was a good man to have in charge, but he was not a lawman and, if push came to shove, he could not be expected to sacrifice his life. Nor would she want him to.

She stopped at a tree-lined creek to douse her face with the stream's cool water and to let her horse drink. She'd been on the trail almost two hours and was satisfied with her progress. In the not too far distance, about twenty minutes away, she reckoned, Belle could see the rocky pass to the south of Clancyville through which she would have to travel. Once through the pass, the trail improved and soon after became a road across flat, easily travelled country.

She vaulted into the saddle. 'Won't

be long now,' she coaxed the tired mare. Belle let the animal find its own way up the far bank of the creek and continued to let it set its own pace, only gently urging the mare on when its gait became too sluggish.

* * *

In the hills above the creek, Barrow and his fellow killers were riding as fast as the treacherous and narrow prospector's mule-trail would allow them to. He cursed the recent rains which had eaten away at the track and had littered it with shale from landslides. Every now and then his horse's footing became uncertain on the shale and made him acutely conscious of the ravine that the trail skirted.

'Come on!' he shouted to his partners, as they slowed their pace and lagged behind, conscious of the bone-crushing death awaiting them if they made a mistake on the winding trail. 'Time is runnin' out. If Belle Black gets safely through the pass, it won't be so easy to stop her in the open country between it and Clancyville.'

Spitter Doyle, constantly chewing and spitting, and the more cowardly of the pair, whined: 'The money in our pockets ain't goin' t' be no good, if'n we go into that ravine, Luke.'

Brad Dannon agreed. 'Spitter's calling it right. My hoss is so slack-legged from ridin' the shit outa him, that he could buckle any second.' His wide, fear-filled eyes glanced down into the rock-strewn ravine and he slowed his pace even further.

'Ah!' Barrow glowered. 'I should have got men to ride with me, not cissies!' He urged his horse forward at a pacy clip up the sharply rising trail, but he was sweating as the soft mud and shale made for precarious progress.

*　*　*

Jack Roycroft poured his best brandy from a crystal decanter into four crystal

138

glasses and then handed one each to Frank Burton, Ben Charles and Wes Shine.

'Everything, gentlemen,' he said, raising his glass, 'is in hand.'

Each man present in the banker's parlour wanted to ask him exactly what he meant, but each man also didn't want to know.

'We'll have ourselves a new marshal today,' he promised them. 'And Stoddard will swing soon after Barrow pins on a badge. Buck Morgan will be pleased. The Big M's business will still be ours.' He put the glass to his lips. 'Here's to continuing good times, gents.'

★   ★   ★

Luke Barrow, impatient with his over-cautious partners, widened the gap between him and them, anxious that Belle Black would beat him to the pass and make it through to Clancyville. Once or twice he rode his luck on the treacherous trail, but his journey ended in a wide smile as he picked his cover in the rocks of the pass, with Belle Black approaching, unsuspecting of the deadly trap she was headed into.

Barrow hunkered down and settled his rifle in a comfortable niche on his shoulder. He waited as the marshal drew nearer, counting the seconds, applying pressure to the Winchester's trigger, leaving only a hair's-breadth to explosion.

'Keep on a-coming, Belle,' he sniggered. 'Keep right on a-comin', gal!'

12

Barrow's partners, fearful of inciting the Big M foreman's rage, which, when full blown was a sight to behold, picked up their pace and arrived in the pass to see Belle Black steadily and unknowingly riding into the trap set for her.

'Get outa sight!' Barrow snarled.

Spitter Doyle, the more jittery of the two, scrambled to cover, not taking the kind of care a man needs to take in rock-strewn terrain if he wants his presence to go undetected. His boot caught on a loose rock and sent it clattering down the slope. Barrow watched in horror as the stone bounced off the boulders, seeming to leap higher with each bounce. Belle Black was some way off yet, but she had ears to hear and eyes to see with. However, Barrow reckoned his luck might be holding when, half-way down the stone skewered off, took one almighty leap through the air, seemed destined to wake the dead when it landed again, but plonked right into a sandy, soft spot and stuck fast. The echoes of its final bounce rattled among the rocks and boulders. Barrow's keen eyes went Belle Black's way to monitor her reaction, and found that there was none. She just kept riding on into the pass, unconcerned.

Luke Barrow glared at Spitter Doyle, and with icy malevolence growled. 'I ought to blast you to kingdom come.'

Doyle, paling, whined: 'Mistakes happen, Luke.'

'Yeah!' Barrow growled, 'you're sure evidence of that, Spitter.'

'No call to insult my ma,' Spitter complained. 'Even if she was a tent-town whore.'

Barrow edged sideways a little. His insult had raised gall in Doyle that might just turn to temptation if he showed his back to the slow-wit.

Belle rode on at a steady pace, conscious of the threat to her well-being. She had not missed a thing, but if she were to turn and high-tail it, she'd make an easy target for the bushwhacker or bushwhackers high up in the pass. Of course it was possible that it was a loose stone, or one disturbed by an animal, but with a plate full of the trouble she had, it was likely to be a two-footed varmint who'd loosened the stone.

While holding her head up, as if her only interest lay in safely negotiating the narrow trail through the pass, Belle's eyes switched every which way, hoping to spot movement or the glint of sun on a gun-barrel. There was nothing. In fact, so devoid was the terrain of any hint of another's presence in the still morning that Belle began to put her unease down to jitters.

It was then she saw a hovering vulture, soon joined by another, then a third and fourth, circling above the pass. Belle reckoned that the birds' instincts were telling them of a fresh meal in the offing. She began to sing a popular ditty that the singer in the Jug o' Grog performed every night, to give the impression that she hadn't a care in the world.

High up in the rocks, Luke Barrow sneered.

'This is goin' to be easy, fellas.' He scratched the black stubble on his chin. 'But just in case, you move along a trot or two, Spitter, to the far end of the pass.'

Doyle, keen to make amends for his earlier mistake, gladly obliged, this time watching every step he took before he took it.

Belle let her horse amble on until she drew almost level with where she had seen the stone bounce and hoped that having seen it through the distorted heat-haze coming up from the floor of the pass, she had not mistaken from whence it came.

She tensed every muscle in her body, ready for action.

Drawing level with the spot, Belle whipped her rifle from its saddle scabbard, spurred her horse, crouched low in the saddle and slung lead into the rocks. Luck favoured Belle, and soured for Barrow. A lucky bullet hit a rock near Brad Dannon, spitefully spun off and ripped off half of his right ear. Howling like one of Hell's demons, the town hooligan leaped up, clutching his ear, blood from the wound streaming through his fingers.

'Git down ya fool!' Luke Barrow yelled.

Dannon's anger kept him standing. 'That bitch gone shot me, Luke,' he screamed.

Belle took full advantage of Dannon's showing to straighten up in the saddle and lay lead in his chest. Laughing insanely, he looked down at the splurge of blood on his shirt-front, pulsing from his pain-wracked chest, before toppling head first from the rocky heights of the pass, arcing out and dropping free for most of the way, until he became impaled on an out-jutting rock with a point sharper than a needle and a shaft more jagged than an alligator's teeth. The pointed rock went through his belly and out his back, sending the circling vultures into a frenzy. They swooped down, and Belle's bullets splattered two of the evil birds against the rockface of the pass, but almost at once the sky was black, the vultures fighting each other for the tastiest morsels.

Luke Barrow had no such respect for his fallen partner, taking advantage of Belle's humanity to send a bullet her way that blew off her saddle horn and spooked her horse. The mare broke into a headlong gallop. Belle was forced to grip the beast's mane in a desperate attempt to stay aboard. If she was thrown, she'd end up with more broken bones than sound ones, if she survived at all.

The Big M foreman and Doyle had

free shooting practice, every ounce of Belle's effort going in trying to calm the mare. A bullet nicked the horse's belly, and all hope of Belle's gaining control vanished. With grim foreboding, she glanced ahead to the off-shoot narrow passage that the horse seemed hell-bent on squeezing through. It was lined on either side with jagged rocks, and barely the width of a horse. She had no choice. She had to gamble. Belle risked life and limb by letting go of the horse's mane to try and grab the trailing reins. Would she be successful or dead?

The next couple of seconds would decide . . .

13

Miraculously, Belle got hold of the reins and steered the horse back to the wider trail that led from the pass. However, Willis Creek's marshal knew that the danger to her was far from over.

'You gone to sleep, Spitter?' Barrow hollered, as Belle succeeded in calming her charging horse's insanity, and was making tracks for the exit from the pass. Belle Black was vanishing in her dust, and his bullets were proving ineffective to stop her.

Barrow's shots buzzed around Belle on her headlong dash, which was fast taking her out of the Big M ramrod's range. But there was still Spitter Doyle to worry about. He was standing on a rock overlooking the exit from the pass, lining her up in his rifle sights, and there was nothing she could do about the danger, as her entire concentration had to be devoted to steering the still-excited mare through the exit. It looked like she was charging right into death. She had seen Doyle shoot in town competitions and knew that he seldom missed his target — static or moving. She would not make it through the pass exit. She had to do something.

Fast!

Belle measured the distance to a sandy patch just up ahead that looked soft and yielding. She wiped away the sweat pouring into her eyes, blinding her. She tensed, ready to fling herself from the horse, praying that when she did she would hit the soft sand and not its rocky perimeter. And that in the sand there were no hidden surprises.

'God dang,' Spitter Doyle cried in open admiration, as Belle took a dare-devil leap from her charging mount. 'You're some feisty lady, Belle Black. It's sure a shame that I have to kill yuh.'

Doyle's first bullet buzzed wide of the mark as it passed the spot that Belle had already left. His second was closer, spitting sand in Belle's face as she lay winded. Forcing breath back into her lungs, she was up and zigzagging for cover by the time Spitter Doyle got off his third shot. His bullet was crossed by Luke Barrow's round as he scrambled through the rocks to close the gap and catch Belle in a deadly crossfire.

Every step for the marshal was pain-ridden, her skin scratched and bruised by the small stones embedded in the sand where she landed. She dived for cover in a tumble of rocks as, again, the pair opened up. Her cover was good. In the lead-filled air, it had to be.

Spitter Doyle, irked by his failure to nail Belle, was the more eager. Scrambling down through the rocks laying siege to Belle's position, he lost his footing. Before he could regain it, Belle coolly stepped out to sink lead in his skull. The top of Doyle's head exploded as the bullet exited his cranium, spewing tasty fragments for the diving vultures to snap up. They were on him before he hit the ground.

Luke Barrow, stunned and shocked by what he'd witnessed, began to dodge upwards to the plateau where he'd ground-hitched his horse. As she hurried after him, Belle Black's bullets chased the Big M foreman. As he vaulted into the saddle one of her bullets smashed his right shoulder, and he screamed in pain like a wounded animal. His screaming continued as he disappeared from sight, down the trail at the blind side of the pass. Belle gave up her pursuit. There'd be time to deal with Barrow when she got back to Willis Creek, if he was still around. It took time to find and subdue her excited horse. Back in the saddle, she thundered out of the pass, across the flat country beyond, and only drew rein again outside Marshal Ben Cade's office in Clancyville. The lawman had already come to the door, alerted by the thunder of Belle's hoofs along Main.

'Hello, Belle,' he greeted, his craggy face curious. 'Is Satan on your tail claiming your soul, gal?'

Belle could not speak for a minute or so until she got spittle in her desert-dry mouth and air in her tortured lungs.

'Marshal Cade. I need one of your deputies, and I need him fast.'

He looped an arm around her shoulders. 'I've got fresh coffee brewing. Come inside and let's talk about what's got you so riled up, Belle. How's your pa keeping these days?'

'I haven't got time for chin-wagging,' Belle said. 'I've got to get back to Willis Creek right away.'

Cade stood back and observed Belle's dishevelled appearance, and the many cuts that her leap from her horse had inflicted on her.

'It ain't like Abe to send you on what seems to have been a dangerous errand, Belle?'

'My father is in Doc Forbes's infirmary with a busted femur, and — '

'You need to get your wind back,' the marshal interjected. He overruled Belle's objections and guided her into the office. Once inside he sat her on a chair and said. 'Now, why don't you begin at the beginning, Belle.'

★　★　★

Jack Roycroft strolled on to the bank porch to enjoy one of the Cuban cigars he had shipped in from San Francisco along with all the other items, like the scented French hair-pomade he used to keep his greyness at bay, leaving only a distinguished shock of grey at the temples. He drew deeply on the rich, dark tobacco, feeling at ease with the world. He had just ended a visit from Buck Morgan that had not been as thorny as he had expected. He'd managed to keep Morgan friendly with his promise to see his son's murder avenged.

'Barrow will be marshal of Willis Creek before the day is out. Then that murdering skunk, Stoddard, will get the swift justice his foul deed deserves,' he'd assured the rancher.

Roycroft omitted mention of the murderous errand he'd sent Luke Barrow on. Buck Morgan, even enraged as he was, would never hold with killing a woman. Once Barrow was back in town, a quick word in his ear would put matters right, and Belle Black's demise would be a mystery. He read men well, as every crook had to, and he was confident that, with Stoddard swinging in the breeze, Buck Morgan's questions would be nil, or easily fielded. He'd have the vengeance he'd come to town to procure and would, Roycroft figured, go back to his ranch from where he seldom ventured forth since his wife's death.

He would get the breathing space for some slick accounting to cover the bank's shortfall in funds until some new investments came good, and he'd be in a position to replace the cash he'd purloined from the bank's customers.

His equilibrium was shattered when, out of a knot of excited townsfolk at the far end of Main, Luke Barrow rode in, low in the saddle, and crashed to the ground outside the mercanttile store. One of the men came running, shouting. 'Doc . . . Doc Forbes.' He hammered on the infirmary door and a testy Forbes yanked it open.

'This door is wood, Ed Benteen — not iron!'

'It's Luke Barrow, Doc,' Benteen said. 'He's shot up pretty bad.'

It was news that Jack Roycroft did not want to hear. He dodged back into the bank, hurried to his office and locked the door. Wild panic gripped him. What kind of a she-devil was Belle Black to have got the drop on Barrow and his partners. He went to the drinks cabinet, dispensed with the fancy crystal glasses and slugged whiskey straight from the bottle. The liquor put some iron back in his legs, but not much. As far as he could see, all he could do now was high-tail it out of Willis Creek, before he, instead of Andy Stoddard, ended up kicking air on a lynch mob's rope.

* ★ ★

Having heard Belle Black's story of the mayhem that stalked Willis Creek, Marshal Cade said regretfully: 'The bad news is, Belle, that I ain't got a deputy to loan you. Eddy James has taken to his bed, sick. And Jed Wood is escorting a prisoner to the penitentiary.'

Belle's spirits flagged. 'I need help, Marshal Cade. And I need it bad.'

'Well . . . ' Cade sucked on his clay pipe thoughtfully, before concluding. 'No.'

'No, what?' Belle pleaded, ready to grasp at any straw.

'Well, there's Rupert Bilberry, I guess!'

'Rupert whataberry?'

'Bilberry. He's English,' Cade said by way of explanation.

'English?'

'Not much good with a shootin' iron.'

Belle wailed despondently.

'But he can sling a knife like no

man I've ever seen!'

'A knife-thrower isn't much good against a bullet,' Belle opined.

'You ain't seen Bilberry use a knife,' Cade said. 'Follow me!'

Belle trailed the Clancyville marshal to the Dirty Cat Saloon, anxious that she was wasting time, and seeing little use in watching a knife-thrower. However, a minute flat after entering the Dirty Cat she had a full appreciation of Cade's admiration for the Englishman, who looked more Apache than English.

Marshal Cade explained.

'Bilberry lived for six years with the Apache. It's from them that he learned his knife-throwing skills.'

Bilberry invited a lanky patron: 'In your own good time, dear boy!'

'Dear boy?' Belle yelped.

'The English talk kinda funny, Belle,' Cade said. 'They go in for a lot of that 'dear boy' kinda stuff!'

The lanky man picked a card from the green-baize table he sat at.

'What card have you chosen, dear

fellow?' Bilberry enquired.

'King o' hearts,' said the man, who would be a sore disappointment to a hungry vulture.

'Throw the card in the air any time of your choosing, dear chap. And I'll sink a blade dead centre of the king's heart.'

The crowd gave a collective gasp, followed by much doubtful head shaking — Belle Black's shaking the hardest of all.

'Yeah?' the lanky man said in awe. 'You're saying that if I flick this card in the air, anytime I like,' he held up the king of hearts, 'you'll stick this critter through the heart?'

'Dead centre, dear boy,' Bilberry confirmed.

'It can't be done,' a beer-bellied man at the bar sneered.

'You're fulla shit, English,' another man yelled.

'Then,' Bilberry said with a confident swagger, 'this should be easy money for you chaps.' He threw a cloth sack of dollar pieces on the bartop. 'That sack contains two hundred dollars that says I can do as I say, dear fellows.'

The Englishman appointed a silk-vested gambler to hold the bets, as men rushed forward to grab a share of Rupert Bilberry's poke.

The lanky man holding the playing-card stood up with the card between his fingers. The seconds ticked by. The tension in the saloon mounted. A couple of times before he finally flicked the card upwards the crowbait man teased the unflappable Englishman. When he did throw it, Rupert Bilberry's right hand moved faster than the eye could see, clutched a stiletto from behind his back from a belt that had several knives in sheaths, and twisting his wrist released the knife in an upwards spin, the blade chasing the card. The slim-bladed knife reflected the light from the saloon chandelier as it whizzed past to pin the playing card to a pillar, its blade quivering.

'Would someone care to check the veracity of my claim?' Bilberry invited.

Belle stepped forward.

'I will.'

The knife-thrower strolled across to Belle and, to her utter astonishment, took her hand to kiss it. A snigger rippled through the crowd. Bilberry held her hand and led her to the pillar to which the playing card was pinned.

'Dear lady, if you would?'

Belle, still mesmerized by the smooth-talking, slick-mannered Englishman, took the card from the pillar. Her eyes popped.

'Witnesses, please,' Bilberry called.

Every man in the saloon volunteered and crowded round Belle. She held up the playing-card. The light travelled through a clean hole in the king's heart. The Englishman was swept up to the bar where he'd be imbibing until he drew his last breath if he were to accept every patron's hospitality. Belle drifted back to Ben Cade.

'I never saw anyone so fast with a knife!'

Cade chuckled. 'Fast? He's having an off night, Belle. I reckon he could take the eye from a fly with a knife.'

'He's fast. But is he faster than a bullet?' Belle questioned.

'This ain't no place for a lady,' Cade advised, as a raucous note crept into the Dirty Cat's celebrations. He escorted Belle back to the law office, explaining as he went: 'Bilberry arrived in town a week ago, just about the same time that a trouble-stirrer by the name of Willy Cross was getting into his stride. He figured that making a fool of Rupert Bilberry, with his strange way of mouthin', would be a diversion from slugging whiskey and bedding doves . . .'

Ben Cade laughed.

'Well, Bilberry took his joshing for a while, before he grew tired of it and told Cross to back off or be ready to pay the price. What price would that be? says Willy. You keep foolin' and you'll find out, Bilberry tells him.

'Now, Willy Cross ain't the bravest feller to ever come down the track, and by now he's seein' the steely glint in this English fella's eyes. So, he slaps Bilberry on the back and says that he didn't mean nothin' and it was only all good clean fun. The Englishman says, OK. But all of that day Willy Cross's humour got meaner, as the acid in his gut from having to back off Bilberry fermented.

'That night, when the Dirty Cat closed its doors, havin' been entertained by Bilberry's knife-tricks, Willy Cross, stinging with resentment at the English feller's popularity, lurked in the alley near Ma Clancy's boarding-house, where Bilberry has lodgings, to even the score by backshooting him. I was on my round and saw the whole thing. Cross snuck out behind Bilberry as he went past the alley, six-gun primed and pointed dead centre of the knife-thrower's back. Now, Willy ain't a heavy-footed gent; in fact he's got feather steps when he needs them. I was about to call out to warn Bilberry, when fast as venom leaving a rattler's fangs, he swung around, fingered a Bowie from that knife-belt he wears, and flicked it at Willy Cross.

'Now, I tell ya, Belle, Bilberry's hand hardly moved, but that knife swung straight to the centre of Willy Cross's heart.' Marshal Cade shook his head in wonder, and admiration, too. 'Willy never got near gettin' off a shot!'

'You know,' Belle said, making up her mind. 'Rupert Bilberry might be just the man to pin a deputy's badge on, Marshal Cade!'

She turned back from the law office door, and headed straight for the Dirty Cat Saloon.

14

Dusk saw Belle and Rupert Bilberry back in Willis Creek. She went straight to Doc Forbes's infirmary to check on her father, and Ace Mooney, too. Though Mooney had tried to kill her, Belle knew that he was not a killing man. He had acted out of heart-festering after Linny Bates's death, and in his grief had lost his senses. She was pleased to hear from Forbes that he'd extracted the bullet and stabilized him.

'He's strong and healthy. I think he'll pull through, Belle,' was Doc Forbes's diagnosis.

In answer to Abe Black's gawking at the strange-looking *hombre* sporting a belt full of knives and a flowing mane of fair hair whom his daughter had in tow, Belle introduced the Englishman.

'Pa. This is Rupert Bilberry. He's come to help us.'

Abe Black clearly thought his daughter had taken leave of her senses. A conviction that was confirmed when the strange *hombre* exclaimed:

'Dear boy, dashed bad luck, eh? Fractured a toe once in a cricket game and found it most inconvenient dancing at the Hunt Ball.'

Forbes dropped the scissors he was holding and they clattered on the floor. He looked at Bilberry as if he'd just discovered an unknown species.

'Mr Bilberry is English,' Belle explained to both men and to Ace Mooney, who was beginning to stir. Sam Forbes was first to regain his voice.

'English, huh? That might explain it, sure enough,' he mumbled.

'Gee, I'm real sorry for tryin' to kill yuh, Belle.' Ace Mooney apologized in a voice as weak as a new-born kitten.

Belle recalled how generous of heart her father had been when she'd come back home with her tail between her legs after seeing Ike Westcoff for what he truly was.

'I guess I can understand why you tried, Ace. Love can do some awful darn things to a body's head,' she said.

'Yuh mean you ain't spittin' mad with me, Belle?'

'Oh, I'm mad — good and mad too, Ace Mooney. It's just that I know you weren't right in the head last night with grief for Linny Bates.'

'Heck, Marshal Black,' the Big M ranny said. 'That's sure some gal you've got for a daughter, sir.'

'I know that, Mooney,' Abe said. 'Known it since Belle was a nipper.'

'You know what I think, Mooney,' Doc Forbes said. 'I think this fever you're running right now has more to do with your sweetness for Belle Black than your wound.'

'Doc!' Belle yelped, colour as hot as hellfire flaring in her cheeks.

'Yuh know, Belle, Doc might just be right.' Ace Mooney's sigh was as close to a swoon as didn't matter.

'Don't just stand there grinning,'

Belle berated the medico. 'Go get that boy something to cool his brain!'

Belle was surprised by the flutter that Ace Mooney's sigh had started in her heart. She'd never reckoned on him as husband material. But maybe that was because she'd never figured on having a man under her feet before?

'Belle, can I talk to you in private?' Abe Black said.

'Sure, Pa.'

'If you'll excuse us folks.'

Alone, Black croaked. 'Where's the deputy you went to Clancyville for, Belle? And in what way can that strange-talking feller help you?'

Belle explained. 'Marshal Cade was fresh out of deputies. So he showed me what Bilberry can do with a knife.'

'A knife is no match for a bullet, Belle,' Black wailed.

'In Rupert Bilberry's hand it is,' she assured him.

He shook his head. 'No man is that good with a blade, Belle.'

'If you'd seen, you'd believe, Pa.'

167

Belle told a disbelieving Abe Black about Rupert Bilberry's knife tricks she'd witnessed in the Dirty Cat Saloon.

Talk of Rupert Bilberry now out of the way, Abe asked: 'Did you shoot Luke Barrow?'

'Had no choice. He tried to bushwhack me. Him, Spitter Doyle and Brad Dannon. Doyle and Dannon are dead.'

'I'll be . . . ' Abe Black hugged his daughter to him. 'You might just have the grit to wear that star after all, gal!'

It was a compliment that made Belle feel over the moon.

'Is Barrow still sucking air?' the petticoat marshal enquired.

'In the next room.'

Larry White, the town news-runner, burst through the the door.

'Abe, the travellin' judge's just rode in.'

Abe Black's eyes went Belle's way.

'That's the kind of news you should be delivering to the marshal, Larry.'

'Huh?'

'Belle's the Willis Creek marshal now.' Abe chuckled. 'And you know what. I'd be mighty careful not to step on her toes.'

'Ma'am,' White doffed his hat to show a hairless head.

'Well, what're you waiting round here for,' Abe Black playfully rebuked his daughter. 'You've got a trial to get on with, gal!'

15

Jack Roycroft and Ben Charles had their faces pressed to the bank window. There was a tremble in the mortgage-lender's voice.

'That's Judge Nathan Speck, Jack,' he fretted. 'Asks lots of questions and runs his court by the book.' The mortgage-lender's worry deepened. 'That two-Colt gent escorting his honour is Julius String, a US marshal. With Belle Black forming a trio, this town might just get hotter than Hades.'

'You hear your skeletons rattling too, Ben?' Roycroft scoffed.

'Speck won't hang Stoddard on anyone's say-so but his own, Jack.' Charles's tongue licked parched lips. 'String's a trained investigator. Spent time with the Boston constabulary learning their new-fangled ways of investigating crime. While Speck judges,

String nose-pokes.'

Charles had visited Roycoft with a proposition which he now put to him. 'You know, Jack, I was thinking that you and me should shake off the dust of this burg.'

'You and me, Ben?' Roycroft quizzed.

'As partners.' He sneered contemptuously. 'There're towns all over this country full of suckers, just waiting for a couple of smart fellas like us to part them from their money.'

'I'm a banker,' Roycroft loftily sounded off.

'And a swindler!'

'How dare you, sir!'

'Just like me,' Charles said. 'I saw the green in your gills when Buck Morgan mentioned closing his account with the bank.' His sneer deepened. 'You were real sickly, Jack.'

Roycroft knew there was no point in protesting his innocence. Being a crook like him, Ben Charles would not be deceived.

The mortgage-lender said: 'Julius

String would be mighty interested in fellas like you and me, Roycroft.' Seeing the banker's Adam's apple bobbing, Charles played his trump card. 'Besides, you don't want to be around when Belle Black finds out that you murdered Linny Bates.'

Jack Roycroft staggered under Charles's hammer-blow. From now on, the mortgage-lender knew that he was pulling all the strings.

'I saw you come through the window at the end of the hall where Linny Bates's room was, and quick-foot it down the back stairs to join the crowd outside the Jug o' Grog. You had more jitters than a bride, Jack.'

'No one saw me!' Roycroft raged.

'I did, Jack,' Charles chuckled. 'And if I didn't, I sure know now that you killed Linny. Because you've just confessed.' Charles helped himself to Roycroft's fine French brandy, pouring generously, and sipped while the banker stewed. 'My guess is, too, that you've been helping yourself to Buck Morgan's cash. I figure you murdered Linny Bates, because she somehow found out and threatened to squeal. You wanted Stoddard to hang quickly, to stop Morgan poking around in the bank's books.'

Quietly, Jack Roycroft said: 'You've got a plan, Ben?'

'Yeah. Simple and straightforward. You clean out the vault, and I'll grab what I can. We'll pool our resources and shuck this town before it's our necks and not Stoddard's in Nathan Speck's noose.'

'They don't hang a man for fraud,' the banker snorted. 'What other skeleton have you got lurking, Ben?'

Ben Charles sniggered. 'A couple of years back I had a partner who . . . well, disappeared.'

Jack Roycroft scoffed. 'Do you make a habit of losing partners? I can't say the revelation makes for easy sleep, Ben.'

Charles scoffed also. 'And you know, Jack. I think I might very well develop insomnia myself.'

'Brandy?' the banker offered.

'Why not,' the mortgage-lender accepted. 'It would be a shame to let good liquor gather dust.'

Pouring the liquor, Roycroft turned his back on his new partner, mixing in a yellow powder that he spilled into the brandy from a cuff-link that sprang open when pressed, to reveal a tiny cavity that contained the powder. There was a familiarity to the action that hinted at previous and possibly frequent use. At any rate, it showed the banker's expectancy of trouble and his ruthless readiness to deal with it when it came along. He handed Charles the doctored drink, and raised his glass in a toast.

'To the suckers of Willis Creek, Ben. And all those yet to come.'

'Amen to that, Jack!'

Roycroft supped, then paused, his brow furrowed.

'Before we leave, there's just one problem I need to take care of, Ben.'

'Luke Barrow?' Charles accurately guessed.

'Yes. If he opens his mouth, he can tell people that it was me who greased his palm to waylay Belle Black. And the law gets mighty persistent when it's one of their own a man pays to plant.'

'What about Barrow's partners?'

'Both dead,' Jack Roycroft told his new, but short-lived, partner, only he didn't know it yet. The brandy he'd given Charles contained a slow-acting poison that he'd used before, when he was in the kind of bind he was in now. He'd got a pouch of the root extract from an old Indian medicine-man for a bottle of rot-gut. It had been a good investment.

★　★　★

'Seems to me that Mr Stoddard is as good as swinging, Marshal!' Having read it, Judge Nathan Speck put Andy Stoddard's statement aside. He had also listened to Belle Black's narrative.

'Either this fella is as honest as the day is long, or, he's a really fanciful story-teller. I reckon the jury will opt for him being a yarn-spinner, Marshal Black.' Speck stood up and stretched his long back. 'In my experience, fellas holding a smoking gun inevitably earn a verdict of guilty!'

Belle fretted. 'I don't think Stoddard is of the killer breed, your honour. He's a tearaway, sure enough. But if tearaways were strung up, there wouldn't be enough trees in the West for all the hangings.'

Nathan Speck held up the statement that Abe Black had taken from Stoddard.

'This tale about Linny Bates being Stoddard's sister and how they met on a Mississippi paddler . . . Well, it sounds to me to be as false as Satan's promises. Then there's this pie-in-the-sky mishmash about his being waylayed by a masked man in the woman's room . . . '

'It's so outrageous it could be true,

Judge,' Belle countered. 'If you give any credence to the adage that truth can sometimes be stranger than fiction.'

String put in: 'Seems to me that you're a champion of this hobo's cause, Marshal Black.'

Belle shrugged. 'I just have this feeling that Stoddard's yarn might be true, and that he's not Linny Bates's killer.'

Judge Speck cast lively eyes String's way.

'I think this might be an opportunity to test your detecting skills, Julius. Go look over the scene of the crime. See what catches your eye.' His attention turned to Belle. 'I suggest you accompany him Marshal. It's your town and your rules. So you have the final say in what happens!'

'Thank you, your honour.' Belle hurried to catch up with the already departed Julius Stringer.

★　★　★

Doc Forbes had just changed the dressing on Luke Barrow's wound when the barrel of a six-gun poked through the open window behind him. On seeing the glint of sunlight on the gun barrel's polished metal, Luke Barrow's mouth opened and closed but only a dry croak came out.

'You take it easy now,' Forbes advised his patient, completely misinterpreting Barrow's wild-eyed stare. Roycroft's gun blasted, nicking Forbes on the shoulder on its way to shattering Barrow's chest. A quick follow-up blasted the Big M foreman's face away.

Belle Black spun round in the door of the Jug o' Grog and sprinted towards Doc Forbes's infirmary, her father's safety uppermost in her mind. She burst through the infirmary door, six-gun primed. Hobbling from his room, Abe Black told Belle: 'Barrow's room.'

Belle hugged the wall and edged towards the closed door. Sam Forbes came close to being his own patient as he lurched through the door, clasping his injured shoulder.

'Someone's got Barrow, Belle.'

Ace Mooney had joined Abe and between them they grabbed hold of Forbes, just as his face turned a dirty yellow. Belle was already charging from the infirmary into the alley that led to the rear of the building, knowing that she was too late. Barrow's assassin would be long gone. Frustrated, Belle paced about, kicking out at anything that came her way, until her eye caught sight of a black smudge, like wet soot, on the window pane. Curious, she examined the stain. Taking the residue of the smudge between her fingers, she sniffed at it. It had a sweet, sickly scent that set Belle Black's heart racing. She had smelled the scent before, and knew from whom.

Belle laughed.

'I'd say that that was a French whiff, Belle.'

On exiting the alley, Belle played a hunch and joined Julius String in Linny Bates's room at the Jug o' Grog, where he'd gone to investigate the scene of the crime, as Judge Speck had suggested.

'What are you looking for, Marshal?' String enquired testily, as Belle rooted through Linny Bates's wardrobe.

'A black mask!'

'There isn't one,' String confirmed. 'It was the first thing I looked for.'

Belle held up a black shoulder-shawl, and draped it over her head and face.

'I think, maybe, I've found the mask that Andy Stoddard said his attacker was wearing.'

To String's surprise, Belle sniffed the shoulder shawl, like a prowling tom might a cat in heat. Her yelp of delight jangled his nerves. Then Belle took to examining the shawl, inch by inch, until she rubbed a smidgen of soot-like compound between her fingers and sniffed it. It smelled exactly the same as the stain on the infirmary window!

'What's that?' Julius String questioned, his curiosity overcoming his testiness.

'French hair-pomade,' she announced. 'And I know just where to find the damn jar it came from.'

16

Ben Charles was sweating like a hog in desert country. He checked his watch for the umpteenth time. It was all of fifteen minutes since he'd heard Roycroft's gun explode, and since then he'd watched with mounting concern Belle Black's and Julius String's activities. His heart lurched dangerously and his breath was getting scarcer all the time. His legs felt as heavy as lead. He watched from the closed bank as the marshals exited the Jug o' Grog, making tracks directly for the bank. His soaring panic snatched away the last of his breath. There might still be time to make it out the back door and along to the livery where there were saddled horses on standby for him and Roycroft. He grabbed the valise that only a short time before the banker had taken from the vault, full of the bank's cash.

The valise would slow him up, but he'd be damned if he was going to leave all that cash behind. On his way out the catch of the valise snagged on the edge of the back door, spilling its contents on the floor. At first Charles went milk white, then sunset red as his anger kicked in, on seeing the files and bank notepaper that Roycroft had stuffed into the valise to fool him. Just then the bank's front door burst open and Belle Black strode through, Julius String on her tail.

String swaggered up to Ben Charles, his light-blue eyes taking in every inch of the mortgage-lender.

'You know, Marshal Black,' he said. 'I reckon I've seen this fella's dial on a dodger some place.' He pondered some more, before concluding. 'And I reckon it was for murder, too.'

Game up, nerves shattered, Ben Charles was not slow to vent his anger on Jack Roycroft, confirming the view already held by Belle that Jack Roycroft was Linny Bates's murderer.

'I saw him leave through the window at the end of the hall where Linny's room was. And the bastard admitted that he was her killer, anyway.' Belle's puzzled gaze went to the contents of the valise. 'That bag was supposed to be full of bank money,' Charles explained.

'Bank money?'

Ben Charles tugged at his shirt-collar, as a greasy sweat rolled down his checks. His voice was slow and croaky.

'Roycroft's a no-good thief as well,' the mortgage-lender bleated. 'He's been robbing his own bank. That was why he had to kill Linny Bates. She found out about his thieving. Linny tried to blackmail him. He was having none of it.'

'Well, that explains why he was so keen to have Stoddard swing for murder. With him dead and carrying the blame, Roycroft would be safe.' Belle asked, 'Did Roycroft shoot or arrange for Luke Barrow to be shot at the infirmary?'

'He did the shooting himself,' the mortgage-lender confirmed. 'He greased Barrow's palm to see to your demise, and wanted no loose ends.'

Suddenly Charles's legs gave out and he crashed to the floor. 'My legs! I can't feel my legs! Get Doc Forbes.'

'The doc is poorly himself,' Belle informed him. 'One of Roycroft's bullets got him in the shoulder.'

'My hands,' Charles wailed, in a dry rasping voice. Then he rubbed his eyes, as if rubbing away sleep. 'I'm going blind!'

'Do you feel as if you're floating?' Marshal String enquired.

'Yeah,' Charles confirmed. 'What the hell's happening to me?'

Julius Stringer had seen Ben Charles's symptoms before, and had heard tell of the paralysing potions that the Indian medicine-men could brew. Wandering the country after the Indian Wars, they were ready to sell their deadly potions to unscrupulous men for a bottle of rot-gut.

'Did Roycroft pour you some liquor before he left to do his foul deed at the infirmary?' Stringer asked.

Charles's voice was now a mere whisper, and his eyes were rolling wildly.

'Brandy.'

Julius String sighed. 'Then I reckon we can chalk up another murder to Roycroft.'

Ben Charles never heard his words. He was already dead, his eyes yellowed by the poison, his face grey and mottled.

The thunder of hoofs on Main got Belle's and String's attention. Belle ran to the bank window to catch a glimpse of Jack Roycroft's tail as he rode out helter-skelter, scattering pedestrians crossing the street.

'I'll get him,' String said, heading for the door. Belle beat him to it, her face set grimly.

'I'm marshal in this town. I'll get him.' A minute later Belle Black was haring after Roycroft, with a whole bagful of scores to settle with the conniving killer.

★   ★   ★

Roycroft beat a trail to the hills south of town, which were still dotted with holes and mineshafts from dried-up claims. Willis Creek had had a loco spell about five years back when a prospector had found a fist-sized gold nugget in the hills and a flurry of digging began. It didn't take long to find out that the prospector's nugget was the only one in the hills, and men went back to ranching and store-keeping and clerking, leaving the hills ugly and dangerous. Almost every other week someone fell down a hidden hole, or the earth crumbled under their feet as the rains ate away at the bellies of the shafts and the earth collapsed inwards to fill the holes. It was dangerous terrain, and under normal circumstances Jack Roycroft wouldn't venture into it. But he was left with no choice.

Fine food and good liquor over the four years he'd been in Willis Creek had expanded his gut and rear end, and his poundage was now a distinct disadvantage when weighed against Belle Black's slim trimness. If he stuck to open country, it wouldn't take long for Belle's nag to outrun his stallion, fine animal though it was. So, his only hope lay in luring Belle into the hills and getting the drop on her. It was a strategy he was pretty certain would work.

★   ★   ★

Belle was wise to the banker's thinking. It didn't take much in the way of brains to figure out that in a straight run, Roycroft's horse would buckle long before hers. That left only one option — the narrow trails and dangerous terrain of the hill country. Belle caught sight of Roycroft heading up through a stand of pine, and knew that from now on she'd need luck on her side.

Roycroft, being first into the hills, could pick his spot, set his trap and wait. She would have to avoid that trap, and a hundred more as deadly, if she wanted to bring Jack Roycroft to book for his crimes.

Roycroft went high into the hills to make his stand. He settled down to wait in a nook overlooking the main trail through the hills, which Belle Black would have to take to the point where he planned her demise, before trails began to offshoot, giving the marshal options. He'd have to kill her before she had the chance of taking one of those trails. Because if that happened she'd vanish from sight for long periods, and trails wound into trails. Roycroft did not know the geography of the hills, whereas he'd bet Belle Black did, and if he let her disappear from sight she might just pop up from anywhere. Another consideration, of course, was time. By now the suckers of Willis Creek would know what godawful fools they'd been, and be as mad as riled rattlers. They'd come looking for him, so he couldn't afford to fool around playing games with Belle Black. He'd want to avoid the sound of gunfire, too. That's why he was lurking behind a boulder, ready to prise it loose the instant Belle Black showed.

Again, Belle was second-guessing the banker, figuring that he'd want to be well out of the immediate territory before a howling mob of men he'd cheated came looking for him. Buck Morgan, for one, could call on fifty men to hunt him down. So Belle figured that Roycroft would try to nail her at the first opportunity, and that would be where the hill trails divided round the bend up ahead. No sooner had she arrived at this conclusion than she heard a rumble as loud as thunder; shock waves vibrated through the overhead rocks, shattering the hills' stillness. Belle glanced up to where a boulder was bouncing down the hillside directly above her, coming so fast that she doubted very much if she would have time to get out of its path. The boulder cracked other rocks open and sent them hurtling out in every direction. Dislodged shale preceded the crushing avalanche; each shard of stone, as deadly as any bullet, hurtled through the air making it thick with menace. It looked to Belle that wherever she dodged, she'd have to have luck on her side to avoid death.

It looked like half the damn mountain was coming down on top of her!

17

Belle reached up, grabbed a tree-branch and hauled herself from leather, only seconds before her horse was swept from under her by the boulder, over the edge of the trail and into a deep ravine. Belle's anger became white hot, as she watched the helpless animal being bludgeoned by the boulder and a thousand other smaller rocks in the deadly cascade released by Roycroft. However, she had to shelve her anger and concentrate on her survival as Roycroft, seeing her survive his master plan, peppered the pine tree with bullets which buzzed around Belle with deadly intent, clipping branches and scattering them every which way, any one of which could dash her from her precarious perch into the ravine after her horse. A secondary landslide thundering down the mountain might also snap the spindly tree and sweep her into oblivion.

Belle could not return the banker's fire, having only a six-gun, which would be useless. Even if her bullets reached the high promontory that Roycroft ruled from, they'd not have the spite left in them to puncture a paper bag! Her Winchester had gone with the horse.

High up in his lofty hide-out, realizing Belle Black's predicament, the banker's panic eased and was replaced by a calculating calm. The tree that the marshal was clinging to was sparsely clad and spindly, trying to survive as it was on the edge of the stony trail, on the fringe of a ravine, unnourished. It wouldn't afford her much cover, so all he had to do, as he saw it, was to shimmy down through the rocks until he was close enough to pick off Belle Black, careful to stay outside killing range of her Colt .45. He'd observed that she hadn't had time to grab her Winchester from its saddle scabbard before hauling herself into the tree.

Maybe, even, another boulder might crush the tree, and sweep Belle away with it as it crashed into the ravine. He had options, choices he wished he could savour and enjoy. But time was against him. He needed to make tracks. Dust was already clouding the distant horizon to the south, and all there was to the south was Willis Creek.

Roycroft sized up a boulder or two but, unlike the one he'd already set rolling, they seemed to be too firmly planted to be so easily prised loose. And even if he put in the effort, which would be considerable and energy-sapping, along with being time-consuming, there was no guarantee that the boulder would not be diverted from its path and leave Belle Black sitting pretty. If that happened he'd still have to get close enough to pick her off.

'So, might as well get on with it right now,' he grinned evilly.

On seeing Roycroft's intent, Belle climbed further up the tree to where the foliage was slightly thicker, but still not plentiful enough to hide her. All she could do was pray, and hope that the banker would come within the range of her six-gun to give her a sporting chance. But that was unlikely to happen. The Willis Creek killer was way too foxy to allow that to happen. She slung a few shots his way by way of protest, but he cockily stood atop a boulder laughing as her bullets fell short, or passed him with a tired sigh.

'Any last wishes, Belle?' he mocked her, as his rifle again began to spit.

To her amazement Belle saw Rupert Bilberry appear out of the rocks to the left of Roycroft, as if by magic. His time spent with the Indians had clearly not been wasted. Not only had he learned to use knives like no man she'd ever seen, but he'd also obviously learned the Apaches' feather-footedness. He had not disturbed a leaf, cracked a twig or moved a pebble as he had crept up on Roycroft.

'I say, old chap,' he said laconically,

hands resting on his hips, 'not very sporting to behave the way you are towards a lady.'

Jack Roycroft spun around, alarmed at first, then he began to laugh uproariously on seeing the gun-free Englishman.

'It's really not the done thing, old bean,' Bilberry said. 'Now, I suggest that you leave Miss Black be, and ride back to town to answer all those questions needing answers.'

Roycroft's laughter turned to a sneer, and he levelled his rifle on Bilberry.

'I wouldn't do that, dear boy.' The Englishman sighed. 'If you want to stay alive, that is.'

'You're on your way to hell, mister,' the banker growled.

A blink would have been a long time, compared to the time it took for a Bowie to flash in Bilberry's right hand and stand quivering in Jack Roycroft's windpipe. The banker gagged, tried to pull the knife free, but hadn't the time to do so before toppling headlong off the boulder to make pulp of his skull on one lower down.

'I believe it's safe to come down now, Marshal Black,' Bilberry called to a stunned, but mightily relieved Belle.

★   ★   ★

Belle and Bilberry crossed trails with the town posse on their way back to Willis Creek. There were two pleasures to calm the angry men; Jack Roycroft's body and the valise stuffed with the town's cash that he'd been making tracks with.

Joey Belham, the posse leader, told Belle: 'All hell's broken loose in town, Marshal. Buck Morgan has lost patience after talking to Judge Speck, and has ordered his ranch hands to town to haul Stoddard to a tree and string him up.'

'Stoddard isn't the one who killed Linny Bates and Randy Morgan. Jack Roycroft is. Marshal String and I proved as much.'

'That fella String tried to tell Buck Morgan that, but he'd set his course by then and there was no pulling back. One of the Big M rannies laid a gun-barrel across String's skull,' Belham added. 'Some of us boys would have helped, at least those of us who wouldn't be for hanging Stoddard. But we couldn't let Roycroft ride free with every penny we own, Marshal.'

'Me and Mr Bilberry need the fastest horses in this posse!' Belle declared. She'd shared Rupert Bilberry's bay, using Roycroft's own horse to carry his body, and the double load had pretty much worn the Englishman's horse out, the beast not being the liveliest to begin with.

'I guess that would be mine and Barney Scott's, Marshal,' Belham volunteered. The posse leader handed over his midnight-black stallion to Belle, while Scott volunteered his sprightly mare to the Englishman. They set off at full gallop, leaving the rest of the posse to eat their dust.

Reaching the outskirts of town they could hear the hullabaloo that forecast big trouble. Racing along Main, Belle drew rein and leaped from her horse to crash through the crowds to face Buck Morgan, whose men had a rope around Andy Stoddard's neck. One of them had his hand raised to slap the hindquarters of the horse that her prisoner was astride, to send him galloping.

Belle pulled iron and warned the man: 'You slap that horse and I'll shoot you right where you stand, mister.'

Buck Morgan growled.

'We've dallied enough, Miss Black — '

'Marshal Black!' Belle grated.

'There isn't any such thing as a female marshal,' Morgan flung back. 'Leastways, not in my book. One of you boys escort the . . . ' the rancher's lips twisted in a parody of a smile, '*marshal* home.' His anger-filled gaze went to

Stoddard. 'Hang him!' he ordered his men.

Belle began to panic as the crowd closed in on her.

'Really, chaps,' Rupert Bilberry's honeyed tone had all heads turning his way, 'you fellows are really rather uncivilized. Now. I'd say that you should all listen to the marshal, and do as the good lady says, like good fellows.'

The crowd's laughter was cut short by another interventionist.

'I second that!' All heads now turned to Abe Black, standing on the board-walk, using a broom as a crutch, toting a primed shotgun. He addressed the rancher. 'Buck, your son was an innocent victim. Marshal String has told me about Belle's and his investigation, and Ben Charles's confession about Jack Roycroft being the murderer of Linny Bates and your son. Randy just happened to be in the wrong place at the wrong time.' His tone softened. 'I know you're grieving something awful, Buck. But if you hang young Stoddard you'll only add guilt to your grief.'

Julius String came from Doc Forbes's infirmary with a bandaged head and a right ear four times its normal size, to tell the crowd the full story of the banker's murderous shenanigans. And how, once Linny showed her hand, he was left with no choice but to kill her to keep her mouth shut, and himself free from her influence for the rest of his days.

'I reckon if you check the bank's records, you'll soon have verification of his dishonesty, and confirmation, too, of his motive for killing Linny Bates, Mr Morgan,' Belle said. 'Roycroft's paid the full price for his deeds.'

Slowly, Buck Morgan's anger waned.

'What'll we do, Mr Morgan?' one of his men asked.

'Cut him loose!'

Four men, partners of Luke Barrow, infuriated by the turn of events, took issue and drew iron. Belle downed the man nearest her and winged a second, while Rupert Bilberry's knives flashed, giving the two remaining men no chance to get off a shot. There was a gasp from the gathering at the speed of the Englishman's blades.

'Thank you Mr Bilberry,' Belle said. She turned to Stoddard. 'You'll have to go back to jail until I talk to Judge Speck, Andy. But I guess this time your stay in the pokey will be a short one.'

Finale

Abe and Belle Black tried to settle back into the way of life around Willis Creek, but their disillusionment with the town was not to be overcome. Finally, Abe answered one of his sister's repeated calls to come East. The Changs, on the end of one too many slurs, had already packed up and left. Buck Morgan was a much poorer man in money, Roycroft's fraud having been even more serious than anyone imagined. More important, he was poorer in spirit. With his only son dead, he had near enough adopted Andy Stoddard, so deep was his remorse for the wrong he'd almost done the young man, and most folk now accepted that when the time came for Buck Morgan to pass on, it would be Andy Stoddard who would be the new boss of the Big M.

Belle Black had never reckoned on

leaving the West. But Julius String had kindly written to the Boston chief of police, and she was on her way to becoming a Boston police officer. String predicted a bright future for her as a detective. Abe Black would be taking up clerking in his brother-in-law's bank. His busted leg had healed but was just about useful enough as a prop, and would always now lag behind his other leg, preventing him from being the kind of lawman he'd want to be. He had decided not to stand for re-election as marshal, and Belle had lost her appetite for wearing a badge, too.

The happenings at Willis Creek had forged new relationships and ended old friendships. One such relationship was Belle Black's warming to Ace Mooney's company. Mooney had fully recovered his strength under Doc Forbes's care, and had gone back truly remorseful to the Big M, where he had taken over Luke Barrow's job as foreman.

Belle, boarding the stage to begin her

journey East found herself looking for a sight of Ace Mooney, but he was nowhere to be seen. Sam Forbes and Joseph Sullivan, the Jug o' Grog's owner, where all the mayhem had begun, saw them off. Frank Burton and Wes Shine came to the stage depot to tender their apologies for their part in the events that had, Belle reckoned, changed Willis Creek for ever.

As the stage rolled across the wide flat plains to the south of town, Abe Black left his daughter with her thoughts. He had thoughts too, and they were centered on the cemetery on a shaded knoll overlooking Willis Creek, where Beth Black rested. He had spent an hour there the day before, explaining to his wife why they had to leave, and he came away knowing she approved. Joseph Sullivan had promised to tend her grave, and Abe knew that he could trust the Irishman's promise.

The thunder of hoofs and the wild yelling behind them had Belle Black leaping from her seat to look out of the stage window at Ace Mooney's wild charge to catch up. He galloped past and grabbed the team's reins, and brought the ancient Concord to a shuddering halt.

'What the hell d'ya think yer doin'?' the driver complained.

Mooney dismounted and opened the stage door to sling an arm around Belle Black's waist and hoist her from the vehicle.

'Belle, I might be the dangest fool that ever left a woman's womb. And if my question gives offence, you just slap my face, get back on board the stage and that'll be an end of it.'

'I will, Ace!' Belle yelped, throwing her arms around Mooney's neck.

'I ain't asked the question yet, Belle,' Mooney said.

Abe Black chuckled.

'Son. I think you've been asking your question in a whole lot of ways for almost six months now.'

'You'll marry me, Belle?' Ace Mooney asked.

'I'll marry you, Ace Mooney,' she said. 'The first second we come across a preacher.'

Mooney cut loose with a wild yell that echoed across the plain. He slapped the Big M horse on its hindquarters to send it cantering back to the ranch. He kissed Belle with a passion that had Abe Black frowning at first, but laughing seconds later as she fought for breath.

They climbed aboard the stage to resume the long trek East. Andy Stoddard appeared on top of a rise to wave to them. Abe Black glanced back to Willis Creek, reflecting on how fickle life could be. Belle and Ace Mooney did not look back. Their happiness had already swept away all thought of the town, and of the past.

Abe wondered what kind of a marshal Rupert Bilberry would make.

We do hope that you have enjoyed reading this large print book.

Did you know that all of our titles are available for purchase?

We publish a wide range of high quality large print books including:
Romances, Mysteries, Classics
General Fiction
Non Fiction and Westerns

Special interest titles available in large print are:
The Little Oxford Dictionary
Music Book, Song Book
Hymn Book, Service Book

Also available from us courtesy of Oxford University Press:
Young Readers' Dictionary
(large print edition)
Young Readers' Thesaurus
(large print edition)

For further information or a free brochure, please contact us at:
Ulverscroft Large Print Books Ltd.,
The Green, Bradgate Road, Anstey,
Leicester, LE7 7FU, England.
Tel: (00 44) **0116 236 4325**
Fax: (00 44) **0116 234 0205**